He looks exactly like a psychic, Kate Yancy thought when she laid eyes on Owen Komelecki.

"It's a matter," Komelecki said, "of focusing on the psychic energy left behind. In this case I will attempt to glean information from the spiritual traces Miss Hampton left."

"I see," Kate said, although she didn't.

He picked up his bulging garment bag and started out to the hallway, then turned and stared straight through Kate and out the window. "There is a feeling," he said slowly, "of . . . death." He stopped, shuddered almost imperceptibly, and tossed Kate a triumphant smile.

She had begun to feel as if she were the ingenue in a Vincent Price movie. . . .

"Deborah Adams brings the rustic wit and wisdom of Lake Wobegone to the plains of middle Tennessee. A delightful mystery from a promising writer!"
SHARYN MCCRUMB

ALL THE GREAT PRETENDERS

Deborah Adams

BALLANTINE BOOKS · NEW YORK

Copyright © 1991 by Deborah Adams

All rights reserved under International and Pan-American Copyright Conventions. Published in the United States of America by Ballantine Books, a division of Random House, Inc., New York, and simultaneously in Canada by Random House of Canada Limited, Toronto.

Library of Congress Catalog Card Number: 91-92186

ISBN 0-345-37075-9

Manufactured in the United States of America

First Edition: January 1992

For EJO, LBL, Glo, and Donald

CHAPTER

1

FROM *THE JESUS CREEK HEADLIGHT*:

SEARCH FOR MISSING GIRL UNSUCCESSFUL

Police Chief Reb Gassler has called an end to the search for Lynne Hampton after an intensive week-long investigation turned up no new information.

Miss Hampton, who disappeared from the Twin Elms Inn in Jesus Creek, reportedly wandered away from the area during the night. Police Chief Gassler would not say whether he believed Hampton had left alone. He did state, however, that Miss Hampton has a history of emotional disturbance and indicated that this could be a factor in the disappearance.

PLANS BEING MADE FOR CELEBRATION

Jesus Creek residents are preparing for the

Sesquicentennial celebration scheduled to begin in early July. A number of events are being planned, and anyone who wishes to participate should contact Edith Nell Moody at the Chamber of Commerce, 296-4420.

By ten o'clock the temperature outside had climbed to ninety-five degrees. Even by Tennessee standards, that was hot. Kate Yancy peeked through the heavy curtains and smiled when she saw the dozen or so reporters wilting in the heat. She considered offering them a pitcher of iced tea but quickly changed her mind.

Oh, if Tom Brokaw were out there, she might give in. But Kate had developed an intense dislike of reporters in general and the ones on her lawn in particular—ever since the black day three weeks ago when they had arrived in swarms to cover the story of Lynne Hampton's disappearance. Interviewing the police had seemed sensible enough, but when they'd started stalking Kate and guests of the inn she'd put her foot down. After that the reporters had managed to garnish every story with one of her quotes. And not the profound ones, either.

She heard a shout from the crowd as a taxi pulled into the long, tree-shaded driveway. Sighing, Kate set her tea glass on the registration desk and went reluctantly to the door to rescue Owen Komelecki, psychic. It took her only one quick glance to realize how little she was needed.

The heat rays that shimmered above the asphalt

drive made the bizarre scene look even more un-
real, as if it might dissolve into a flashback any
minute. Komelecki stood on the taxi's hood while
the driver cowered inside. Kate figured he had to
be Komelecki, because he looked like a psychic. He
wore a purple silk shirt with full, flowing sleeves.
His beard was neatly trimmed and black, except for
two identical gray patches on either side of his
mouth, and he had those eyes, commonly described
as piercing, that one expects in a psychic.

Cool as a cucumber in this heat, Kate thought.
He's a better man than I am.

Holding his arms over the crowd as if to bestow
a benediction, Komelecki smiled tolerantly while
the reporters fired questions at him.

"What do you expect to find?"

"Have you had any visions about the Hampton
girl?"

"Who's gonna win the Super Bowl?"

There's one in every crowd, Kate decided.

From his makeshift platform Komelecki began to
address the crowd. His voice was smooth and controlled, as if it were some sort of instrument carefully played. Though he was speaking quietly and
competing with the mobile PA system a half block
away, he had no trouble making himself heard.

"Please, please," he urged. "I understand that
you're eager to find Miss Hampton. And I'll answer
all your questions soon. But my first priority is to
acquaint myself with this place"—he paused long
enough to wave one arm dramatically toward the
inn—"and absorb the essence of it. I promise to keep
you informed of every development as it occurs."

Komelecki took a moment to look skyward, as if he expected the essence of Twin Elms to fall on his head, then he hopped down off the car like a macho television detective. He threw a garment bag over his shoulder and started up the cobblestoned walk toward the inn. Reporters and curious locals surrounded him, shouting questions and snapping pictures. Komelecki smiled and kept walking.

When he stepped up onto the wide front porch, Kate held out one hand. "Hello, Mr. Komelecki. I'm Kate Yancy."

"Of course," he said, taking the proffered hand and bending forward to kiss it. Kate thought at the time that his mustache tickled. Later she would decide that this pretentious gesture, like almost everything else the man did, had been purely for the benefit of the reporters.

Kate stepped inside and waited in the front hall for Komelecki to follow her. He did, but unfortunately so did the hot, clinging crowd of strangers. Before Kate could recover and slam the door the inn was filled with people, all of them thrusting microphones and cameras at Komelecki.

For one frightening moment Kate stood paralyzed, remembering news reports of innocent bystanders crushed to death by stampeding mobs. "Excuse me," she said politely, trying to wiggle past them, but no one seemed to be paying attention.

"Hey! Excuse me?" she tried again, this time elbowing a photographer out of her way. With all the shouting, and Komelecki's attempts in his soft-spoken way to calm the maddened media, Kate didn't seem to be making much headway.

"At what point were you called in?" someone asked Komelecki.

"Are you working with the police, or does the family want an independent investigation?"

"Excuse me!" Kate shouted. She'd decided good manners had their limitations. She stomped a foot and pushed someone out of her way. If she could just get enough space cleared so that she could open the door . . . There! At least she could breathe. Now if only she could manage to get them outside.

Inspiration struck. Pointing out the door, she shouted, "Good Lord! Isn't that Lynne Hampton out there?"

Reporters flocked to the porch, forgetting all about Komelecki. "Where? Where?" they demanded, and started snapping pictures without bothering to frame or focus. Kate had only to give the ones in back a good shove and they all toppled out on top of each other. All except one, and he clung stubbornly to the door jamb.

"Out, pal. Before I get nasty." Kate gave him an extra nudge in the back.

"Will you stop that?" he shouted, gripping the door tighter.

"Get out!" Kate shouted back.

"Look, lady. I don't know who the hell you think you are, but I've got a reservation here."

"Reservation?" Kate loosened her grip. "You mean you're a guest?"

"That's about it." He glared at her.

Pulling him inside, Kate slammed the door and

locked it. "I'm sorry. I thought you were one of . . .
them." She pointed to the camera hanging around
his neck.

"I am. But I also happen to have a reservation.
Now are you going to let me check in, or do I have
to go to Howard Johnson's?"

Komelecki had watched the whole exchange,
smiling like a parent at bickering children. Before
Kate could recover, he jumped to her defense.

"Please don't hold Ms. Yancy responsible for this
misunderstanding. I'm afraid I've created a bit of
chaos."

The photographer examined Komelecki carefully, then turned defiantly to Kate. "Can I check
in, or what?"

It wasn't what she'd call a sincere apology, but
under the circumstances it would have to do. "Of
course. Now are you Carl Jackson? You sounded
older on the phone, and I wasn't really expecting
you until late."

"I found a shortcut," he snapped.

Ignoring him as best she could, Kate went on.
"But we do have your room ready. If you'll both
come into the study, I'll get your keys." If she'd
been braver—or if she'd been the real manager of
the inn instead of the receptionist—she'd have suggested he go elsewhere. Someplace warmer, perhaps. But people weren't exactly lining up to stay
at Twin Elms, and her brother would be ill as a
hornet if she offended even the rudest of guests.
He'd shake his head and lecture her about responsibility, as if she actually *had* any around the place.

Despite Carl Jackson's impatient foot-tapping

and Komelecki's disarming smile, Kate managed to get things squared away. When she held out his room key Jackson snatched it from her hand, grabbed his shabby overnight bag, and stomped out into the hallway and up the stairs.

"I hope he winds up in the linen closet," Kate said between clenched teeth.

Komelecki leaned casually across the counter and smiled. "I'm sure Mr. Jackson will recover."

"I hope so," Kate sighed. "The way this day has started . . ."

"I sense that you're disturbed by my presence." Komelecki was still smiling.

"Oh, no," Kate quickly assured him. "Anything that helps us find Lynne is worth a try, no matter—"

"No matter how crazy? No, don't be embarrassed. Most people are wary at first, but only because they don't fully understand. I hope to change your mind before I'm finished here."

"You don't have to worry about me," Kate said. "I want to find Lynne as much as anyone does."

"I have no doubt we'll discover what happened to Miss Hampton. Were you able to assign me to the room she used?"

"No problem," Kate said and handed him the key. "First door on the right at the top of the stairs. You know, you're the first psychic I've ever met. How does it work? I mean, how do you know about people you've never even seen?"

Komelecki took a moment to consider her questions. "It's a matter," he said slowly while stroking his beard, "of focusing on the psychic energy left behind. In this case I will attempt to glean information from the spiritual traces Miss Hampton left."

"I see," Kate said, although she didn't. "Do you go into a trance or something?"

He gave her a tolerant smile. "Something like that. Meditation is always useful. It allows me to attune myself, to become more aware of the universe and the powers that surround me. Do you meditate?"

"Who, me? No. I mean, I never have." Kate stuck her index finger through the wedding band she wore on a chain around her neck and began to twist it. This man was strange. Really strange.

Komelecki nodded. "Perhaps we can arrange instruction for you while I'm here." He picked up his bulging garment bag and started out to the hallway, then turned and stared straight through Kate and out the window. "There is a feeling," he said slowly, "of . . . death." He stopped, shuddered almost imperceptibly, and tossed Kate a triumphant smile.

She had begun to feel as if she were the ingenue in a Vincent Price movie. Any minute now the lights would flicker and—

"It comes to me at odd moments." Komelecki continued across the room and up the stairs.

What a performance, Kate thought. Could he really have sensed Anne's death? She shook her head and reminded herself that it was not a good idea to dwell on the ravings of lunatics. Reaching for her tea, she knocked the glass across the desk and watched helplessly as the wet stain spread across the receipts she'd been sorting. She'd just spent an entire morning separating them into piles, and now she'd have to spend at least that much time drying them. A morning's work shot to hell.

The Jesus Creek Sesquicentennial was expected to be the biggest event since Secession. Residents from all corners of Angela County were planning to attend the celebration, possibly to see just how big a wingding the county seat could pull off.

Jesus Creek had originally been named the county seat because it was centrally located. The fact that the entire town consisted of four miles of main highway intersected by a handful of residential streets concerned no one. It was still the largest town in the county.

The Chamber of Commerce and several community groups had planned at least half a dozen events to coincide with the Sesquicentennial festivities—including the Goober Gala, the first ever Jesus Creek beauty pageant, and a fund-raising auction. Businesses and individuals were getting in on the action, too. Mr. Pate, owner of Pate's Hardware, had festooned the front of his store with red-white-and-blue streamers, while The Drink Tank had introduced a Ladies' Night special: Frontier Beer.

In a rare burst of community spirit Kate had volunteered to head the auction committee. Proceeds, she'd been told, would benefit the City Beautification Fund, sponsored by the Jesus Creek Women's Guild. Mind you, Kate had never been a member of that worthy organization. And the fact that none of the members would take the job should have told her something, she now realized.

Of the ten women who'd cheerfully agreed to help, four had come down with sudden illnesses ranging from appendicitis to "a funny feeling all over," two had had to leave town on unexpected personal business, one gave birth, and two simply refused to answer their phones.

Still, it was a worthy cause. Kate supposed she'd have to make the best of the situation, much like the woman whose husband thought he was a chicken. They both needed the eggs.

Never mind that she was already filling in for the itinerant manager of the inn, one Patrick Mc-Cullough, while he roamed the country doing whatever it was small-town mayors did. And never mind that she was taking on a great deal of the maid's duties as well, so that Glenda could prepare for the upcoming Miss Goober Pageant. And forget all about the fact that she had her own job to do, which involved enough work to keep her busy any day. Actually she'd been considering locking herself in her room and putting out a sign reading DEPRESSED, DISTRESSED, AND REGRESSED.

Kate's first stop that afternoon was Eloise's Diner. Eloise, bless her soul, was the tenth and only active auction volunteer. She also served the best corn bread in town.

"Here's my list," she said, shoving a small notebook and a cup of coffee across the counter to Kate. "Pate's Hardware is donating folding chairs, and I'll provide the coffee. Merchants who've offered to donate auction items are listed, along with what they've donated, the retail price, and the suggested starting bid."

"I owe you," Kate said sincerely, and sipped her coffee. "If I had one more like you, I'd be ahead of the game."

"Just remember, you still have to pick all this stuff up and get it to the gym. I feel for you, but not enough to help." Eloise winked her carefully mascaraed eye. "And listen, kid. I know how much free advice is worth, but you ought to get in there and kick a few butts."

Kate nodded in agreement. "I should. I'm a terrible supervisor. How did I get this lousy job, anyway?"

"You're a soft touch. Not that that's so bad. But sooner or later, you've got to put your foot down."

"You're right. And I will. But first, can I have lunch? I haven't eaten all day."

Eloise tossed her Clairol blonde hair and laughed. "When are you going to hire a cook who can cook?"

"I wish I could. But Patrick, curse his name, won't stay home long enough to discuss the problem with me. Besides, he wouldn't dare fire Mrs. Bradford. It wouldn't look good to sack a preacher's wife—and he thinks I should just ignore her, since she only comes in for a few hours in the morning."

"Uhmm. I guess that's one of the drawbacks to being in politics. Gotta stay on everybody's good side."

"Yes, but why should *I* have to suffer? I didn't even vote for him." Kate glanced at the menu. "Meat loaf and browned potatoes."

"You didn't vote for your own brother? What's this world coming to?" Eloise wrote down the order and passed it through the serving window to the cook, then propped her elbows on the counter. "So. I hear your psychic turned up this morning. What's he like?"

"Outrageous," Kate promised. "He's like something from a cheap movie. You'll have to come over and meet him. He wears silk shirts and he kissed my hand."

"Is he cute?" Eloise was currently single and looking to change that.

"I don't think I'd call him cute. Come see for yourself."

"Maybe I will. Just to take a peek. I've never had my hand kissed. But I want to see which way the wind blows before I start flying."

"What do you mean?" Kate asked.

"Honey, you're crazy if you think the Bradfords will let this go by."

Kate shook her head. "I don't know what you mean. Let what go by?"

"Your psychic. You mean you haven't heard the rumblings?"

"Mrs. Bradford had gone home by the time the excitement started. And just for the record, he's not my psychic. He's the Hamptons'."

"Well, I'm surprised that your distinguished cook hasn't mentioned it already. Their whole congregation has been carrying on about this guy coming into town. I think it's silly, myself, but I get a lot of business from those Traditional Faith folks, so I don't want to make them too mad. You sure Bradford hasn't said something to you?"

"I try my best to avoid her," Kate said. "I wonder if we could start having breakfast catered."

"I don't see why not. But it sure would be simpler to make Patrick hire a cook who can cook."

Kate nodded. "I agree. The trouble is, Mrs. Bradford thinks she *can* cook."

Eloise threw her head back and laughed, then turned to collect Kate's lunch order from the serving window and placed it on the counter. "Eat while you can, kiddo. The way things are shaping up, you may lose your appetite real soon."

The worst part of collecting the donations for the auction was stepping outside to put them in the van. The heat would have been torture enough, but there was also the crackle and squeal of the public address system. Set up directly in front of the *Headlight* office, it amplified a series of preteen voices that rattled off Biblical passages with all the emotion of a sunstruck lizard.

As part of the Sesquicentennial observation, Mrs. Bradford had concocted the idea of having the students of the Christian School read orally from the Bible. Fine, Kate thought, but wouldn't fifteen minutes a day do? Did they really have to go on from sunup to sundown? Kate worried about poor old Mr. Proctor, who ran the corner gas station on Main Street and was therefore outdoors all day long. And Constance Winter, who spent every day roaming the sidewalks and passing out baked goods to anyone who'd accept them. How did those people stand it?

Half the merchants on Eloise's donations list had been checked off, and Kate considered taking their merchandise to the gym before she picked up more.

It wasn't really necessary—the van was a long way from being full—but the school gymnasium was a good two miles out of earshot of the Bible-reading.

Looking up, she saw the Bradfords heading down the sidewalk directly toward her. Well, they'd already seen her, so there was no alternative but to stop for a few minutes and speak to them.

"Kate!" Brother B. called out. "Hello, Kate!" He was moving down the sidewalk, slim and dapper in his expensive suit, with Mrs. Bradford close behind.

"Oh, hi," Kate said breathlessly. She hoped to convey an urgent need to be on her way. "How are you folks?"

"Fine, fine," Brother B. said heartily. "Life is always good when you've got the Lord in your heart." Leora, his stony-faced wife stood behind him, arms folded across her chest, as if she were ready to back him up should Kate disagree.

"Well," Kate said, unable to call up any other (socially correct) response.

"Kate, I wish you'd reconsider your misguided hospitality." Brother B. had begun to rock back and forth, as if suddenly seized by a rhythmic spirit. "This blasphemer cannot be allowed to infiltrate our community."

"I'm sorry, Brother B. I don't know what I can do. The Hamptons hired Mr. Komelecki, and surely you understand they just want to find their daughter."

"If only they would put their trust in the Lord instead of this . . . heathen."

"The man is very well known," Kate said soothingly. "I understand he's solved a bunch of missing person cases. And really, he just wants to help. I've met him, and I promise he hasn't got evil intentions."

"That doesn't change the fact that he is practicing evil." Brother B. pulled a dainty handkerchief from his pocket and mopped his forehead. "All this may seem innocent to you, Kate. But I assure you, I've seen dreadful consequences grow from similar blasphemy. Why, members of my own church have been possessed by demons after only the slightest contact with this sort of unholy horror."

"Members of your church? You mean, someone here in Jesus Creek?" Kate tried to imagine any of the locals vomiting pea soup.

"No, no. Other churches in other towns. But it *could* happen here. The power of evil is stronger than human will. Folks get caught up in this nonsense; they treat it like a game, and pretty soon they forget to remind themselves it's bad."

"Really *possessed*?" Kate said, still fascinated with the idea. "You mean, talking in strange voices and gyrating their heads? Brother B. . . . have you ever done an exorcism?"

Brother B. was momentarily flustered. "Well, no. I mean, that isn't how it's done. We pray for the afflicted soul, you see. But we can't always fight the power of Satan. He is the Master of Deceit, and he leads us into darkness. We must be ever on guard against his wickedness!"

Kate hoped Brother B. wasn't drifting into a sermon. "I'm sure Komelecki will be gone soon," she said soothingly. "Speaking of which, I'd better get going. I'm in charge of the auction, you know. I hope you'll both be there."

"The reverend has tried to warn you." Mrs. Bradford had been so quiet that Kate had almost forgotten she was there. "If you refuse to listen, then we can't be responsible for the evil this man unleashes."

"Well, I do heartily appreciate your advice, Mrs. Bradford. But I'm sure Mr. Komelecki will do his job and be gone in no time."

"I hope you're right, Kate." Brother B. gave her a mournful, doubting look. "And I hope to see you in church Sunday," he added with a bit more cheer.

It was almost dark by the time Kate finished unloading the auction items. She returned to Twin Elms to find reporters still loitering on the lawn. Fortunately they were too wrung out from the heat to do more than give her a few limp waves.

The phone was ringing as she stumbled through the front door. Kate kicked off her shoes before picking up the receiver. "Hey, Sis." It was Patrick, of course. Who else on a day like today? "I've been trying to get you for an hour."

"Glenda had to leave early," Kate explained. She slumped across the desk, thoroughly exhausted. "And I've been working on the auction. Glenda's not going to stick around here forever, Patrick. Before she leaves you ought to hire an extra maid, while there's still time for Glenda to train her."

"You bet," Patrick agreed smoothly. "Just as soon as I get back."

"What do you mean? You're supposed to be back *tonight*. Don't you dare do this to me again!"

"Now, Katherine, you get upset about the silliest things. I'll be there Friday. You can hold down the fort another couple of days."

"Don't call me Katherine. And no, I cannot hold down the fort, not with Indians coming at me from all directions. I've got to have that auction ready to go by Saturday. I still have donations to pick up, and the entire gym has to be decorated. That psychic person is here, and the front yard is crawling with strangers doing Lord knows what. And by the way, the Bradfords are furious about Komelecki being here. I'm telling you, I cannot deal with this."

"You've got to develop more self-confidence." That was Patrick. A truly supportive sibling. "Now, here's why I called. I want you to get hold of Sheila and tell her I'll be in Friday night. She'll have to pick me up in Nashville; it's Flight 1103."

"Okay," Kate said, jotting down the number. "What time?"

"I don't remember offhand. Just tell her to check at the ticket counter. I'm sure it's after five P.M. though."

"Well, Patrick, I don't think Sheila will want to hang around the airport all night waiting for you."

"Oh, she won't mind. Sheila's a great gal. Talk to you Friday." He hung up.

Kate wondered if Sheila would be such a great gal if she could hear the giggling coming from Patrick's end of the phone.

Carl Jackson came charging down the stairs just in time to see Kate Yancy throwing a shoe across the room. "I thought you Southern women were too genteel for temper tantrums," he said, coming to a quick halt in the doorway.

Kate glared at him.

"Actually, I've been looking for you," he went on. "We got off on the wrong foot earlier. And it may have been partially my fault. So to apologize, I'd like to take you to dinner."

Partially his fault, my hind leg, Kate thought. But she prided herself on her tolerance and rationality. "Fine," she said, gritting her teeth.

"Where's the best place for cheeseburgers?"

Kate sighed. "Eloise's. Just up the street on the courthouse square. Help me find my shoe and we'll go." She thought she detected a smirk as he bent to pick up the shoe that had landed under a wing chair. Slipping it back on her foot, she told him, "We'll go across the highway and cut through a few yards."

"Can't we take your car?"

"I don't have a car," Kate explained, "just my brother's van. It's a pain to drive anytime, but especially on Wednesday nights."

Carl waited for an explanation but was finally forced to ask, "Your van gets the night off?"

"What? Oh, I see." She realized Carl was from out of town, but it hadn't occurred to her that he wouldn't be familiar with Wednesday night tradition. "Wednesday is church night. Lots of traffic. It's easier to walk."

By the time they'd crossed the first neighbor's yard, Carl had exhausted his supply of small talk. Kate refused to fill in the silence, on the grounds that he was apologizing to her and should therefore be responsible for initiating conversation.

"So," he said, after a few minutes, "tell me about your charmingly bucolic community."

"What would you like to know?"

"Let's see," he droned thoughtfully. "What do you do for fun around here? Organize the Sadie Hawkins dance? Call hogs to dinner?"

"Why don't you go delete yourself?" Kate said sweetly.

"Sorry. I didn't realize how loyal you are to your little town. Okay, then. Where did the stupid—uh, where did the name come from?"

Kate still didn't like his attitude, but she supposed he was trying to be civil. Some people never could get the knack of it. "The story is that a group of religious dissenters left their community up north, looking to settle their own version of Paradise. When they got here the leader, a Mr. Wicken, said 'Unload the mules,' or words to that effect. And they all waded into the creek and baptized each other. So then the settlers who were already here started to call it Jesus Creek. I don't know what it was called before."

"And the town got the same name. Not very creative, were they?"

"Unlike you people," Kate said under her breath.

"Excuse me? We people?"

"You reporters," Kate said impatiently. "From the experiences I've had lately, I'd say you all make up the news as you go along. I mean, newspapers are just as sleazy as—"

"You're not a reporter, are you?" Carl interrupted.

"Of course not."

"That's what I thought. But you're sure you could do the job better than the rest of us."

Kate tossed her head indignantly. "I could at least do it honestly."

"So basically what we're talking about here is this: you said something stupid, saw it in print, and decided to blame it on some innocent reporter who simply did his job."

"I did not. Some jerk twisted what I told him in confidence."

Carl snickered. "You're too old to be that naïve."

They'd reached the diner, and Carl stopped to hold the door for Kate.

"Thank you," she said, storming past him, "but even at my advanced age I'm perfectly capable of opening doors."

"A libber. I should have known. Try to be a gentleman and they stomp on your face." Carl headed for a corner booth, still muttering about thankless women. He slid in without waiting for her.

Eloise spotted them immediately and hurried over to the table with menus. Kate noticed she'd put a little extra swing into her walk. "Well, well," Eloise said in her breathless voice, "is this your psychic, Kate?"

"Him? He's just a reporter."

Carl turned, smiling, to Eloise. "Carl Jackson," he said, extending his hand. "Very nice to meet you."

Eloise cocked her head to one side and smiled,

giving just a hint of eyelashes batted. "I'm Eloise," she said. "I hope you're going to be around here for a while."

"What do you want to eat?" Kate asked, wondering if she'd have to kick Carl to get his attention.

"Cheeseburger," he mumbled, still gazing at Eloise. "Fries. Milk."

Milk? Kate hadn't expected him, of all people, to be the wholesome type. "I'll have the same, Eloise. Except for the milk. Make mine a Coke."

"What kind?" Eloise asked automatically.

"Pepsi," Kate said. "A large one."

Eloise wrote the order, while managing to look through her thick black lashes at Carl. "Just take a minute. Now don't you go away, hear?" She swished back into the kitchen, leaving Carl gaping like an adolescent until she'd disappeared behind the swinging kitchen door.

"Now that," he said at last, "is a woman."

"Eloise could chew you into tiny pieces. Anyway, shouldn't you be sticking close to Komelecki, instead of hitting on women you barely know?"

"Why?"

"Isn't that why you're here? To cover the story of the psychic who is trying to find Lynne Hampton?"

Carl grinned. "Since you brought him up, let's talk about Komelecki." He flipped open a pocket notebook and took out an expensive pen. "What was that business today? This guy is supposed to be a pro. His act this morning looked like something from a cheap carnival."

Kate shrugged. "I guess that's how psychics act.

Besides, the Hamptons are strange people, so it figures they'd hire a strange psychic."

"Judging by *The Inquisitor*," Carl agreed.

"The what?"

Carl looked at her closely. "Don't you read the tabloids? That's one of the biggest ones in the country. All the news, before it happens—that's what they're known for."

"I don't even peek in the checkout lane. Those are the trashiest—hey, wait a minute. You don't work for one of *those* rags? Good grief, go torment some celebrity and leave me alone."

"Actually I work for *The Benton Harbor Sun*, but I read the tabloids and HEIRESS DISAPPEARS FROM HAUNTED HOTEL is a story that needs more coverage."

"That's not a story. That's ridiculous. Exactly what I was talking about."

Carl shrugged. "You're saying the girl did not disappear from a locked room?"

"Sure, the door was locked. But the window was wide open."

"So you think she went out the window and . . . what? Slid down the rainspout or something?"

"In fact, there isn't one outside that window," Kate admitted. "But she could have jumped. It's only on the second floor, and she looked pretty athletic to me. People in movies do it all the time."

"Did it occur to you that someone might have provided the girl with a ladder?"

Actually, it hadn't. Kate had gotten as caught up in the story as some of these reporters, and yet she had failed to consider this perfectly logical explanation. "Yes, of course I've thought of that," she snapped.

"What about it then? Boyfriend? Someone the family wouldn't approve of?"

Kate shook her head. "Why would she check in just to leave with a guy?"

Carl ran his finger along the deep edge of the Formica-topped table. "Why *did* she check in? Had she stayed at the inn before?"

"No, I'd swear she's never been here before. I don't know why she picked us. My brother seemed to know her, though. Maybe that's it—she was just on vacation from . . . whatever she does, and wanted a quiet place to stay."

"Sure. Every little heiress wants to summer in Jesus Creek."

Kate had to admit that he had a point. The Hamptons owned an estate near Nashville, as well as a chateau in the Smokies. Lynne could easily have gone to either of those places. Given the rumored worth of Mr. Hampton—never mind Lynne's own financial status—she could have purchased her own county! "Okay. But her own family said she was nuts. Who knows what she was thinking?"

"Suicide?"

"Don't be morbid. Besides, if she'd wanted to kill herself she could have done it without leaving the room." Now there was a frightening thought. Kate could imagine the ghouls who would have been hanging out on the lawn if some tabloid had proclaimed: SUICIDAL HEIRESS DIES IN COUNTRY INN.

Eloise brought out their burgers, then slid into

the bench next to Carl. "So you're a reporter," she said sweetly. "Which paper do you work for?"

"Benton Harbor Sun," Carl answered. "But I'm on leave of absence right now. Working on a major project."

"Do you know any of the people who work for other papers? Like *The World News Hotline*?"

"Is that the one that sponsors Vampire Watch?" Carl asked. "With the toll-free number?"

"Oh, please." Kate rolled her eyes in disgust. "I can't believe people read that garbage."

"What do you read?" Carl demanded. "Barbara Cartland?"

"I do not. I read educational books."

"Try the romances," Eloise insisted. "They might do you good."

"Yeah," Carl agreed. "That Cartland broad could teach you a lot about how women are supposed to act."

Eloise leaned closer to Carl. "I've got to see about these other customers, but I'll get right back to you." She winked and hurried to the counter for more coffee.

"Now," Carl continued, referring to the entries in his notebook, "I hear there was blood all over the room."

"Do you really read Barbara Cartland? How else would you know what she writes or what she can teach?"

"Blood," he repeated firmly. "All over the room."

Kate decided not to pursue the lit-crit debate— she would reserve the subject of Carl's unexplained knowledge of romances for another time. "There was a little blood on the window sill. Like she'd nicked her finger or something. Was that in some tacky paper, too? God, I can't abide reporters."

Carl snickered.

"You don't count. But if you ever use my words in print," she warned him, "I will hunt you down and kill you in a most unpleasant way."

"By any chance, are you a suspect in this case?"

Carl had turned his attention to eating and flirting with Eloise. Kate found the entire display slightly nauseating. Really, she thought, a grown man shouldn't drool like that.

On the return walk to the inn he was all business again. "So what's your theory? What do *you* think happened to Lynne Hampton? You're in the best position to know. And I suppose you were one of the last people to see her."

Kate shook her head. "I really don't know. I've tried to come up with a halfway sensible explanation, but I haven't found one yet."

"What happened the day before she took off? Anything out of the ordinary?"

"She checked in," Kate snapped. "How should *I* know if she did anything unusual? I barely know the woman."

"What about the other guests? Did any of them talk to Lynne or behave as if they knew her?"

"There weren't any other guests. Except Roger Shelton, of course. And Roger doesn't socialize. He's a charming, fiftyish gentleman and stays up in his room, doing model car inventory."

"You have one guest who never comes out of his

room, is that right?" Carl stopped to add to the jottings in his notebook. "Sounds like a suspect to me."

"Trust me. He's not. Roger has thousands of dollars worth of model cars—some he never even takes out of their boxes—and he's far too busy turning those into slot cars to take time out for criminal activity."

"How about Lynne? Was she depressed, nervous, what?" Carl waited, pen poised above the pad.

"Jittery, I guess. But maybe she's just the high-strung type. I keep telling you, I don't know Lynne well enough to know what's abnormal for her. I would have said—What the hell?"

As they rounded the nearest house and started across the highway, Kate could see that the front of the inn was bathed in light, but not from the security floods Patrick had had installed. There was a crowd on the lawn, each person holding . . . no, not torches, Kate thought with relief. They were holding flashlights and singing, in several different keys, "The Old Rugged Cross."

"What is that?" Carl asked.

"That," Kate explained, "is Brother Eubie Bradford and the entire congregation of the Jesus Creek Traditional Faith Church."

"And is there some significance to that particular song?"

Kate shrugged. "Beats me. I guess it's the only one they know all the words to."

CHAPTER

2

KATE'S FIRST THOUGHT HAD BEEN TO RUN through the middle of the crowd and shout obscenities. It was probably fortunate that Carl had grabbed her arm and pulled her around to the back of the inn before she could get herself into trouble.

"Never get involved until you're sure what's happening," he had advised, and shoved her in through the back door. "We'll go to the study and look out the window."

Now they stood shoulder to shoulder, peeking through the heavy curtains like Nick and Nora Charles. Why was Kate surprised to see Komelecki standing on the porch and singing along with the crowd?

"Can you believe this guy?" Carl sounded as if he admired Komelecki's audacity.

"He just doesn't realize how seriously these people take their mission," Kate whispered. "He may find himself closer to the spirit world than he expected."

Kate could see Brother B. and wife in the front row. They were dressed for church, so she assumed they'd gathered the congregation after services and led them here.

When the singing finally stopped Mrs. Bradford gave her husband a firm nod, then turned to glare at Komelecki. Brother B. stepped confidently up onto the porch and raised his arms to the crowd for silence.

"This man is a sinner against God!" he began, pointing at Komelecki's chest. "I beseech thee, sinner, turn away from wickedness and accept the Lord into thy heart."

"Why do preachers talk like that?" Kate asked. "I mean, he doesn't go into the bank or the grocery store and say, 'Thank thee for thy service.'"

"Is this one of those churches that burns books?" Carl asked. "I've heard you Bible-belters are notorious for stuff like that."

"You've heard wrong. All the churches here are perfectly rational. Brother B.'s church is just a little ... conservative. But even they don't burn books."

"Brother B.'s church, you say? Does he own it or something?"

Kate nodded. "Sort of. He established the church when he came here about three years ago. And he's a nice man. The members of Traditional Faith probably regard him as a father figure. He and Mrs. Bradford do a lot of work around town—helping charities, visiting the sick."

"Sounds like a cult to me." Carl moved closer to

Kate in order to get a better look at the action on the porch. "This should be fun. Watching Komelecki and the preacher square off."

"Sir, you have misunderstood," Komelecki was saying confidently. "I am here to assist in the search for a young girl. It is God who has given me the power of sight and the ability to help unfortunates like Miss Hampton."

" 'The prophets shall become wind, and the word is not in them.' " Brother B. had reached for his handkerchief, and Kate noticed the beaded sweat across his forehead. " 'Thou shalt not hearken unto the words of that prophet!' "

"He must have gone through the Bible and stockpiled the relevant passages," Kate muttered.

The crowd shouted "Amen!" and pushed closer to the porch, but Komelecki held his ground, an easy smile floating across his face.

"I think we'd better go out there and rescue him," Kate said.

"Komelecki's doing fine, if that's who you mean," Carl insisted. "Keep watching."

She would have ignored Carl and rushed to Komelecki's defense, but she'd just recognized the wail of a police siren. Kate had no doubt it was headed their way.

"Oh, great. Someone's called the cops."

"Hallelujah! They'll send the mob home and restore order."

Kate couldn't help herself: she snorted. "You've obviously mistaken our police force for—oh, hell! It's German."

Deputy Chief German Hunt slid the patrol car to a stop in the middle of the street without cutting off the blue lights or the siren. He jogged through the crowd and up the steps, gun, ammunition, and assorted police paraphernalia jingling around his waist.

"All right now. Just settle down." German was shouting to make himself heard above the wailing of the siren.

Mrs. Bradford had followed him onto the porch and joined the small cluster of men there. Every time the blue light of the police car flashed it flitted across her face, making her resemble a badly prepared corpse. "Officer, the reverend insists that this disciple of Satan be removed," she told him, jerking her head toward Komelecki. "It's your duty to protect the citizens of this town from the likes of him."

German hooked his thumbs in his gun belt and rocked backward on his heels. "You must be that famous psychic," he said to Komelecki. "Now, what's all this about?"

Before Bradford could spout an appropriate Scripture, Komelecki started to explain. "I am here only—"

"Hold on a minute." German turned to the crowd and shouted, "Somebody shut off that damn siren!" Somebody did. "That's better. Now tell me what's going on."

"Officer Hunt," Komelecki continued, after checking German's name tag, "I've often been able to assist in police investigations. Of course, the Hampton family called me in, but I'm certain they'd expect me to cooperate fully with you. Obviously if there had been any physical evidence you would have found it. However, I deal in spiritual clues, such as vibrations of the aura, lingering traces of—"

"Yeah, yeah. But what's going on here?" German nodded at the restless crowd.

"I think these fine people have simply misunderstood my reason for being here." Komelecki smiled tolerantly and stroked his beard.

"He's a servant of Satan," Brother B. insisted, not a bit swayed by Komelecki's smooth explanation.

German spit a stream of tobacco juice off the side of the porch and onto the azaleas. "Well, preacher, I don't think there's a thing you can do. S'long as this fortune-teller's not breaking the law, he's in good shape."

"Your policeman seems to have everything under control," Carl said, moving away from the window. "Too bad. A riot would have made news."

"Control? German hasn't even mastered basic body functions yet."

"Are you one of those late-blooming hippies? Hate cops just because they're cops, I'll bet. Or do you still refer to them as pigs?"

"I do not," Kate said, somewhat defensively. "I simply dislike German because he's got the brain of a gnat and wears a gun on his hip. He swaggers around town fighting imaginary ninjas. Does that sound like a man you'd want protecting your life and property?"

"What's the matter? Where's your sense of humor?"

"Oh, sure," Kate said irritably. "You think this is hilarious. But you don't have to live here. I've known German all my life, and believe me, the man has no business being a cop."

"Then why doesn't someone get rid of him?"

Kate shrugged. "He's just a deputy. Reb Gassler is in charge, and he's perfectly normal. But Reb is on vacation or something this week. German takes it all very seriously. I don't even think he's supposed to work night shift, but he just loves driving that car around with the siren blaring."

Outside, the crowd had begun to drift away. Brother B. was spouting Scripture to no one in particular. Mrs. Bradford was still standing solidly behind her man, occasionally echoing his homilies and diatribes. German, leaning against one of the porch columns, was working up another spit. And Komelecki was stroking his beard and smiling benignly.

Finally Brother B. drew himself up and made one last pronouncement. "I have endeavored to warn all of you. Now all I can do is pray for your redemption."

With that he took the steps two at a time and, followed by his obedient wife, led what remained of the Traditional Faith congregation down Main Street and back to town. As they disappeared from Kate's line of vision, she heard the beginning of a ragged version of "Amazing Grace."

German shook his head, said something quietly to Komelecki, and went back to the patrol car. Kate was relieved that he hadn't decided to come in for a visit.

When Komelecki sauntered through the front door and glanced into the study, he looked as if he'd just won a war. "Hello, Kate. Mr. Jackson," he said coolly.

"They're going to hound you to death," Kate warned. "I can tell. You're the church project now."

"Kate's right," Carl said. "Looks like they're on to you, Komelecki. You'd better get out of Dodge City before sundown."

Komelecki was not amused. "I'm afraid this can't be rushed. The spirits speak in their own time. And your attitude will not encourage them. Can't you feel it?" Komelecki splayed his arms theatrically. "Can't you feel the grief of those you hurt with your skepticism?"

"Have it your way, then," Carl said, and shrugged. "But even these rubes around here aren't going to fall for the act. Good night, Kate." He turned and pounded out to the hallway.

"Your friend has a negative attitude," Komelecki said when Carl had gone. "I've found that that sort of person can often react violently in the most unlikely situations. You might want to keep an eye on him. And it wouldn't be a bad idea to purify the inn after he leaves. Do you have fresh herbs?"

"Uh, no," Kate said. "But Mrs. Bradford has a box of cinnamon in the kitchen."

"I'll give you some incense, then," Komelecki said, and smiled. "Burning it will appease the household gods."

Then he went upstairs and left Kate standing alone in the study, wondering what the heck had just happened.

* * *

Thursday morning Kate woke early, acutely aware of the feeling that it was going to be one of those days. She took her time dressing, pulling her long hair into a cool and functional ponytail and slipping into cotton slacks and a T-shirt.

Roger Shelton was in the hallway at the bottom of the stairs when she finally ventured out of her room.

"Good morning, Roger," Kate said as cheerfully as she could at that hour. "Having breakfast with us?"

"You know I live for danger, but I'm in a hurry. There's a show in Nashville today, and I want to get there before everything's picked over."

Roger was an avid collector of model cars. He had been living in a half-finished room for two months now, simply because it was the largest and he needed the space for storing his collection.

"We're going to have to give you a separate room, just for your cars," Kate told him.

"I've been thinking about that. No, seriously. I expect to be out of your hair soon. There's a batty old lady over on West Main with a garage apartment for rent. I've decided to take it. The current tenant is supposed to be out in a couple of weeks."

"I suppose that's good news for you. Frankly, I hate to see you go. You're the only sane person I talk to these days."

Roger reached out to pat her arm. "You're in serious trouble if you think I'm sane. Nevertheless, I promise to visit once in a while. I'll have to. You're the only one in town who'll speak to me."

Kate nodded sympathetically. Roger had arrived from East Tennessee two months before, expecting to retire quietly to this small river town. Unfortunately, he'd spent most of his first week in Jesus Creek unknowingly insulting the very people who were most likely to have become his friends. In a town that takes its history personally, Kate had explained to him finally, it was not a good idea to expound upon one's personal theory that Nathan Bedford Forrest was a drunken, illiterate bigot with a penchant for penicillin.

"Have you met the psychic yet?" she asked.

"Haven't had the pleasure. Will I like him?"

"No," Kate said. "But as a favor to me, will you promise *not* to say the first thing that pops into your head when you do meet him? Carry a pen and paper, if you must, and write down your comments. You can show them to me when we're alone."

"Now there's an idea. I could sell my witty quips to a magazine. One that appreciates literate humor." Roger reached around to pat himself on the back. "For now, though, it's off to the races." He picked up two boxes full of assembled model cars, which he'd be racing in Nashville. "I'll bring home a trophy tonight. Count on it."

The dining room was directly across the entry hall from the study. With the doors wide open Kate could easily hear voices coming from inside. She wished she'd stayed upstairs.

"You don't fool me," Mrs. Bradford was saying.

Kate peeked in cautiously. Mrs. Bradford stood in the middle of the room, pointing her finger accusingly at Komelecki. "Jesus is in my heart, and

He helps me recognize demons like you. The reverend says we'll fight you until the battle is won."

Komelecki held his hands out to her, palms up. "Dear lady, I assure you that I am no demon. Any power that I have is God-given."

"I don't expect you to admit it. But you'd better understand that we're on to you. The reverend says if you're smart you'll get out of here right now. Before the Lord takes care of you Himself." Trembling with anger, Mrs. Bradford whipped out of the dining room and into the relative safety of the kitchen.

"I'm sorry," Kate said, crossing the room to Komelecki's table. "Please excuse her. She's . . . excitable."

"Merely frightened." Komelecki didn't seem to be the least bit ruffled. "Many exist in a darkened reality."

"Still, you're a guest here. She owes you a certain amount of respect. I'll have a talk with her."

"She's afraid of freeing her soul to its inevitable destiny. Don't give it another thought. I can handle Mrs. Bradford."

Kate was stuck for a reply, so she simply asked Komelecki if he'd had breakfast. "Maybe I could join you," she suggested. "I'll tell Mrs. Bradford we're ready to order."

Kate entered the kitchen, mentally reviewing the steps outlined in *Mega-Management*. Befriend your employee. Deal with every situation calmly. Be firm.

Mrs. Bradford was at the work counter, driving her fist into a lump of biscuit dough. The light from the window was shining through her thin gray hair, and Kate stared for a second at the outline of the woman's skull. It was fortunate, Kate thought, that Mrs. Bradford was beyond petty vanity.

"We'd better get something straight," Kate said, louder than she'd meant. "Mr. Komelecki is a guest. You will treat him with some amount of respect."

Mrs. Bradford spun around to face her. "I've got no respect for Satan or his agents." Her curled upper lip implied that she had no respect for innkeepers who sheltered them either.

"If you can't treat the guests decently, then I suggest you find another job. Now Mr. Komelecki and I are ready for breakfast." Kate left the kitchen feeling proud of herself for having stuck to her guns, and a little guilty for hoping that Mrs. Bradford would take offense and quit. Surely that is the most irritating woman, she thought. Can't cook, can't get along with anybody, and she's such a bossy old witch.

Komelecki was sitting in one of the ladder-back chairs, gazing gently into space. When Kate returned to the dining room he managed to drag himself back to the real world, then jumped up and pulled out a chair for her.

"Why, thank you," she said, sitting down. "We don't get many gallant guests."

Komelecki bowed slightly before reseating himself. "A beautiful woman inspires gallantry."

Not certain how personally the compliment was intended, Kate smiled and said nothing. She'd never been all that confident about flattery, even when it was blatant.

"I have news that may interest you," Komelecki whispered. "About Lynne. Last night I had what you might call a vision."

"You're kidding." Kate winced at her poor choice of words. She had the feeling Komelecki took his work very seriously.

"And I am certain that she wants to be found. It seems that Lynne is—"

"Secret society?" Carl had ambled in and helped himself to the third chair at the table. "Morning, Kate. What are you and your resident loony up to today?"

Kate made a face at him. Komelecki, however, ignored the insult. "Actually, Mr. Jackson, I think you'll be interested in this. I have information about the Hampton girl."

Carl leaned casually back in his chair without taking his eyes off Komelecki. "Do you?" he asked skeptically.

"Indeed. And here's Mrs. Bradford." Komelecki tilted his head to one side and peered around Kate. "Perhaps you'd like to be in on this, too, Mrs. B."

Mrs. Bradford was bearing a tray filled with menus, a coffeepot, and two cups. She pretended not to have heard. "I'll get another cup," she said tersely, motioning to Carl.

"Never mind," Komelecki told her. "I don't drink coffee. It clogs the system with impurities. I'll have fruit and water. Bottled, if you have it."

"We don't."

"Tap water will suffice, then."

Carl took Komelecki's cup and filled it from the pot. "Blueberry pancakes," he said after studying the menu briefly. "My system doesn't mind being clogged."

"Cereal," Kate said. She'd already learned that Mrs. Bradford's pancakes could clog most anything.

Having taken the breakfast orders with a dour expression, Mrs. Bradford left the dining room without speaking. Kate guessed she was making her best effort to tolerate Komelecki. Well, it would have to do.

"So you've got a lead on the Hampton girl, have you?" Carl was clearly looking for an argument this morning. "Go ahead. I'd love to hear all about it."

Komelecki turned to Kate. "I'll need your cooperation. I have several methods for obtaining information in cases like this. At this particular time I believe trance-channeling would be most effective. My spirit guide has expressed a willingness to be present tonight. Perhaps we could use the study?"

Carl laughed and slapped the table. "That's great! I wondered if you'd get around to the old channeling routine."

Kate had listened carefully, trying to extract something from the context of the conversation. It hadn't helped. "Forgive my stupidity, but what is channeling?"

Komelecki was about to respond, but Carl beat him to it. "He's going to stage a séance. Only they don't call it that anymore. *Trance-channeling* is the new jargon. This should be a hoot."

"You want to hold a séance in my study?" Kate nearly choked on the words, but unfortunately they were still distinct enough to assault Mrs. Bradford as she came through the door.

"Oh, Mrs. Bradford, I—" Kate began to explain. But the poor woman merely slammed Komelecki's fruit tray down on the table and stormed back into the kitchen. Kate sighed. "We may have pushed that woman toward her grave. Do you really think a séance is a good idea?"

"I have already received substantial information. But a channeling session is the fastest way to pinpoint the exact location. My guide has access to facts that could lead us directly to Lynne Hampton."

"Let him do it," Carl urged. "I haven't had a good laugh in a while."

"This is not for your amusement," Komelecki told him sternly. "Our purpose is to help another human being. After all, Mr. Jackson, we are ultimately responsible for each other, as all of us together compose the cosmic soul."

"Excuse me," Kate interrupted, "but can't you just do this in the privacy of your own room and give us the results later? Why does it have to be in the study?"

Komelecki stroked his beard thoughtfully. "I feel very strongly that those on the other side want a group to be present. You see, they work in strange ways. Strange to us, that is. Their purpose is greater than any of us can imagine. And even as they provide information about Lynne, they will also be using our presence for purposes of their own, to enlighten. I'd like to have you there, Kate. And the Bradfords."

"You're joking, right? You don't think the Bradfords will agree to participate in a séance?"

"Trance-channeling," Carl reminded her.

"I'm convinced that, given the opportunity to experience for themselves, they will realize I present no danger."

"Who else?" Kate asked suspiciously.

"No reporters," Komelecki promised, apparently reading her mind.

"Aw shucks, as the locals say." Carl moaned in mock disappointment. "You mean I can't join the fun?"

"You, Mr. Jackson, are very welcome. But I warn you, you may have to change your philosophy afterward." Komelecki leaned back and peeled a banana with an air of satisfaction.

Mrs. Bradford didn't reappear until after the conversation about channeling had ended; Kate wondered if she'd been listening at the door. When she did return, she served Carl without undue courtesy and hurried back to the kitchen. It seemed to Kate that the woman might actually be frightened of Komelecki and whatever powers she attributed to him.

Carl was still trying to choke down his pancakes when Komelecki excused himself. "I'm sorry to have so little time to share with you, Kate, but I must consult with the police this morning." He started to leave, then turned back to ask, "Would there be a health food restaurant in town?"

"Well, no. But Eloise at the diner does serve salads and vegetables."

Komelecki smiled and raised one hand in a sort of regal farewell.

Carl looked up from his coffee. "Maybe Eloise will clog his system for him."

"I don't understand you at all," Kate told him. "If you want an interview with the man, then you'd better start acting civil."

"I told you, I'm not interested in Komelecki."

"Well, what are you interested in?"

Carl leaned forward and propped his elbows on the table. "Think hard now. I'm a writer. Lynne Hampton is a subject. Does that conjure up anything?"

Kate shook her head. "Komelecki is part of the story, right? Don't you have to include him?"

"Sure. But that part I can write without even being there. These guys are all alike. Same routine. Shall I tell you how the channeling session will go?"

"No. Just tell me exactly why you're here."

"I want a story that will make me famous," Carl said simply. "An exclusive."

"So you expect to find some piece of evidence that everyone else has overlooked—your own surprise ending?"

Carl nodded. "While all these other jokers are running around after Komelecki, I'll be digging up dirt on Lynne."

"And suppose you don't find anything? Then you'll have blown your chance with Komelecki, and you won't have any story at all."

"I'm flattered that you care." Carl gulped the last of his coffee and put down the cup with a triumphant flourish. "But I will find something. One way or another."

Glenda Richmond had won all the beauty pageants that Angela and the surrounding counties had to offer. Not only was she frighteningly pretty, she had a natural feel for the walk, the clothes, and the chitchat; she could respond to the standard pageant questions in her sleep. So Kate had been understandably surprised when Glenda applied for the job of maid at Twin Elms.

"Look, Kate," Glenda had confessed, "the work doesn't thrill me. But the hours are good and the pay is reasonable. I can practice pivots behind the vacuum and I can practice singing while I dust. And I may as well tell you, as soon as I win a pageant with a scholarship attached I'll be out of here before you can sneeze."

Kate had hired her on the spot.

She was waiting in the study when her amazing maid arrived on Thursday morning. "I've got something for you," Kate said proudly, and held out a book.

Glenda took it and read the title aloud. *"Winner Take All."*

"It's about beauty pageants," Kate explained. "The author won about a dozen of them. There's an entire chapter of tips on swaying the judges."

"Well," Glenda said with a near sincere smile, "thank you, Kate." She tucked the book into her purse.

"You're welcome. Now use it and win!" Kate would have added a *rah-rah-rah* but decided to suppress her enthusiasm until after the pageant.

"Is Mr. Shelton still in his room?" Glenda asked. "He hovers over me while I'm trying to clean."

"He thinks you're going to injure one of his cars. At least he doesn't chase you around the bed."

"True." Glenda reached into the pocket of her jeans and pulled out an elastic band, then secured her long blond hair with it. That hair was an astonishing product of three shades of Nice-n-Easy and strips of aluminum foil. The other pageant contestants probably spent a small fortune for professional coloring and didn't look half as good.

"How's the auction shaping up?" Glenda asked.

"Slowly. All my ostensible helpers are nowhere to be found, although there was a rumor that one had been sighted at K mart strolling arm-in-arm with Elvis." Kate sighed. "And Patrick won't be back when he said he would. I've got to organize these papers for the accountant. . . ."

"Maybe if you didn't throw them all into a box?" Glenda suggested.

"Plus there's this pack of reporters hanging around, trying to get to Komelecki. I tell you, Glenda, I'm going to lose my mind soon. You may find me running amok through downtown Jesus Creek, vandalizing parking meters or throwing bricks through the library windows."

"That's been done." Glenda shook her head disapprovingly. "Try to be original."

"By the way, Glen, let me change the sheets for the next few days. Just until the pageant. You'll break a nail for sure."

"I can glue on a fake one," Glenda said. "Who's the maid here, anyway?"

"But it's only for a few more days—"

"Kate, relax. One fingernail doesn't make that much difference. By the way, I met your psychic down at the police station this morning."

"What on earth were you doing in the police station?"

"I stopped by to see German. He has a great gym set up in his basement and he lets me use it for workouts. This psychic is a sleaze, by the way. Have you noticed?"

Kate frowned. "I wouldn't say *sleaze*, exactly."

"Yes you would. He smells like sleaze, he talks like sleaze. Somebody should teach him a few new opening lines. 'Didn't we meet once in a previous life?' doesn't exactly make the ten-best list of ice-breakers."

"You're kidding. Did he really say that?"

Glenda nodded. "I told you he was sleaze."

It was late evening before Komelecki returned to the inn. Kate saw him through the window as he strode up the cobbled walk. Before ascending the steps the psychic paused and stared straight ahead. Kate wondered if another vision had accosted him, then she moved quickly away from the window and curled up in a chair.

"Hello," she said when he finally came through the door. "Did you learn anything from German?"

"Ah, Kate. You look comfortable. You *belong* here," he said.

"I do?"

"Absolutely. Your aura is totally compatible with the inn's. Oh yes, a building can have an aura. All the fragments of emotions, the spirits of those who have passed through here . . ." He held out his arms. "All these things collect and color the atmosphere."

"I see," Kate said. It was a deeply romantic idea, and she loved it. Not that she was particularly sentimental, she told herself, and she couldn't imagine why the thought of antebellum lady ghosts floating through the rooms appealed to her.

Komelecki settled into the chair next to hers, his back perfectly straight. "It's a secure feeling, isn't it? To recognize that all those who have gone before remain with us, as a part of our lives."

"I suppose," Kate admitted. "But I'd feel more secure if they weren't so vague. Why don't they just pop in and tell us what we should do and how to solve our problems?"

"They do," Komelecki said firmly. "The problem is, we often fail to listen. You must pay attention to that voice—your own Higher Self—and trust it. Believe that you are all-powerful?"

"Who, me? Mr. Komelecki, I get lost on Main Street. If I were all-powerful—"

"You are. But you must accept the truth of it. Have you ever heard of visualization?"

Kate shook her head.

"You can use visualization to achieve anything you desire. Imagine yourself as you wish to be. Specifically, of course. For instance see yourself, in your mind's eye, counting your money. Go over your assets one by one, those you already have as well as those you wish to have. Very soon your life will begin to conform to this visualized image. Opportunities will present themselves, and you, because of your increased awareness, will be able to grab them."

"Okay," Kate said slowly. "But what if someone

else wants something that's in direct opposition to what I want? Do I visualize that person falling off a cliff?"

Komelecki looked horrified. "No, no! That's a negative concept. You must concentrate on the positive aspects. Don't be discouraged. With time and perseverance you will achieve what is best for you. Obstacles will melt away."

"This sounds too easy. You mean, if I just fantasize—excuse me, visualize—then whatever I want will come true?"

"Yes. Absolutely."

Kate studied his face, trying to determine his capacity for charlatanism. He certainly seemed sincere, and he wasn't trying to sell her anything, after all. "I guess I could try it, except that I don't know what I'd want. I'd hate to waste this newfound power on something trivial."

"If it's important to you, it isn't trivial. It's your desire, your happiness that makes you a complete person."

Kate made a mental note to try visualization that night. After the séance the spirits should be more alert, she figured, and ready to help.

Carl and Kate were the first ones in the study for the channeling session. "Komelecki wants everyone in a circle," Kate told him. "Come on, you can help me move this." She grabbed one end of a love seat.

"Why don't we all sit on the floor?" Carl suggested.

"Oh, hush up and lift."

Another love seat and two wing chairs completed the arrangement. "That should do it," Kate said, gasping. "I don't suppose the spirits concern themselves much with decor."

"Can we turn on the lights now, or are you too tight to use electricity?"

"Komelecki wants them off. Something about his concentration. He said nine o'clock, though. By that time it's going to be pitch-black in here. I don't know. . . ." Kate looked around for an unobtrusive light source.

"How about the desk lamp?" Carl asked.

"We'll try it. Maybe he won't mind."

Carl switched on the lamp, then opened the front door in response to a hesitant knock. "Glad to see you left the flock at home, reverend," he said, recognizing Brother B. from the front-porch gathering of the night before.

Brother B.'s face registered a quick flash of amusement but Mrs. Bradford, standing behind him, glared at Kate over her husband's shoulder.

"Hello. Glad you both could make it," Kate said, and waited for lightning to strike her.

"Good evening, Kate." Brother B. took her hand and shook it firmly.

Mrs. Bradford was somewhat less cordial. "This is an abomination in the sight of the Lord," she intoned. "The reverend was right; you're serving Satan here tonight."

To her credit Kate did not comment on the sulfurous viands served at the inn, food that certainly *was* suitable for Satan.

"Everybody have a seat," she said quickly. "Watch your step, though. It's pretty dark in here."

"The Devil always cloaks his evil in darkness," Brother B. mumbled, and settled into a chair. Mrs. B. continued to stand near the door, as if planning a hasty retreat. She jumped a good foot when the door was flung open by Roger Shelton.

"Hail the conquering hero," he said. "Did they turn off the electricity?"

"Sorry, Roger," Kate said. "We're having a séance, and the lights have to be turned down low."

"It's a channeling session," Carl corrected.

"Really?" Roger looked around the room and spotted the Bradfords. His eyes began to gleam. "Mind if I stay?"

"The more the merrier," Kate told him. "Get comfortable."

After setting his boxes of model cars on the floor, Roger took a chair next to Brother B. "I've just won first place in three different events," he said to the preacher. "You got a minute? I'll tell you all about it."

Kate couldn't bear to watch. Brother B. was one of the first residents Roger had insulted upon his arrival in town. It was hard to get the details straight now that the incident had been embellished by a dozen people, but apparently Brother B. had approached Roger on the sidewalk and asked if he'd been saved, to which Roger reportedly had replied, "No. I'm waiting for the going out of business sale before I buy my indulgence."

Carl dropped into a love seat, spread his legs out

in front of him, and patted the empty space beside him. "Kate?"

She had no intention of playing kneesies with this jerk, but just then German barged through the door. He'd long held the notion that he was welcome in Kate's home and so never bothered to knock. "Hey there." This greeting was followed by a burp. "I heard we're gonna raise the dead tonight. Sounds good, huh Kate?" He winked at her.

Kate bolted over to join Carl, quick to embrace the lesser of two evils. "I didn't know you'd been invited, German."

He had sprawled across a chair, and now was running his fingers up and down the crease in his uniform shirt. "Komelecki dropped by the PD this morning. Said he had some kind of lead on that girl." He pulled a pouch of Red Man from his pocket, stuffed stringy black leaves into his mouth, and began surveying the room for a makeshift cuspidor. "You got a coffee can or something?"

"I don't think so," Kate said hopefully.

"No problem. I'll just hold it in. This won't take long, will it?"

"You sure I'm not in the way here?" Roger asked of no one in particular. In desperation Brother B. turned defiantly away from him and began an exhaustive inspection of the drapes.

"I expect Mr. Komelecki will be delighted to meet you," Kate said. "But I hope you won't feel obliged to comment on the occasion."

"Who, me?" Roger demanded with a self-satisfied smile.

"How long are we going to stand around here?" Mrs. Bradford asked irritably.

"I'm surprised you're here at all," Carl said. "That public demonstration last night made it clear you don't approve of Komelecki or his methods."

"We certainly *don't* approve. But if that man insists on forcing his evil presence on our fellow townsmen, the reverend says it is our duty to stand against him."

"Oh, lighten up," Carl told her. "Tonight's just a parlor game."

"It's a dangerous game. There's no telling what damage might be done." Mrs. Bradford seemed to have become the mouthpiece for the Jesus Creek Traditional Faith Church. Certainly her husband was unusually quiet tonight.

"I quite agree, Mrs. Bradford. It is dangerous to involve ourselves incautiously with the spirit world." Komelecki had entered the room so quietly that no one had heard him.

He was clad in dark trousers and a black silk shirt; in the dimly lit room his head appeared to be floating in the air. On a chain around his neck there seemed to be a chunk of glass. Crystal, Kate would learn later from Carl, who was familiar with its alleged ability to enhance intuitive power.

Komelecki nodded to Kate, then settled gracefully into a wing chair. He leaned forward, elbows propped on the chair arms and fingertips touching lightly. "Let me explain what is about to happen. When I go into a trance, a discarnate will speak through me. In order that we may know we are not dealing with demons"—he paused to glance at the

Bradfords—"all transmissions will be filtered through my spiritual guide, Ham-Ata-Arum."

German grunted. "This guide of yours must be a foreigner. What kinda name is that?"

"Indeed." Komelecki stroked his beard thoughtfully. "Ham is from a world alien to most of us. He is what we call a solity. That is, a single entity composed of the talents and wisdom of several discarnates. He functions as a teacher at this time, guiding and instructing us."

Neither of the Bradfords commented. German had leaned back in his chair, and Kate thought he might be dozing off.

"Ham will be the first to speak. Any of you may ask questions but, please, only one voice at a time. Now if all of you will clear your minds, we will begin. Let peace and harmony flow through you. Join me now in singing the sound of the universe."

Komelecki began chanting, slowly, "Om-m-m-m-m-m."

Only Kate and Roger joined in. Again and again Kate let the word fill her mouth like a balloon, and then she forced it out. It's fun, she thought, this universal sound. Never mind Mrs. Bradford's disapproving grunt.

Komelecki, still chanting, leaned back and placed his palms lightly on his thighs. His voice deepened and Kate thought she saw a ripple run through his body.

Except for the chanting and German's snoring, the room was silent. No coughing or shuffling of feet. Komelecki's breathing suddenly became shallow, and Kate realized she was the only one still chanting. She finished the "Om" she'd started, then grew quiet to see what would happen next.

Komelecki's eyes popped open. "We are here," he—or rather, *someone*—said, for it wasn't Komelecki's smooth, controlled voice. Kate felt a chill at the back of her neck. This voice was loud and firm, and the words emerged in a quirky cadence, as if they were unfamiliar to the speaker.

CHAPTER

3

"WE ARE HERE," THE VOICE REPEATED. "Who seeks us?"

"Who are you?" Carl asked.

"We are Ham-Ata-Arum, counselor to the incarnate Owen Komelecki."

Well, this is shameful, Kate thought. A spirit guide from the astral planes comes to visit, and no one has the decency to offer a word of greeting.

It was Brother B. who pulled himself together first. "Why do you present yourself as a creature of God?" he asked timidly.

"We are all of God. Some lesser, some greater in understanding."

Brother B. wasn't buying that. "The Bible says 'Ye know not what manner of spirit ye are of.' "

"The writings referred to collectively as *Bible* have been corrupted in translation by men who knew not. Would you like the correct translation for that passage?" The voice emanating from Komelecki seemed to be gaining strength.

"Not from the likes of you!" Mrs. Bradford took a step forward, and for a moment Kate thought she might attack the psychic. Fortunately she seemed to have second thoughts and dropped back, fists clenched at her sides.

Komelecki's eyes were open, and he sat perfectly still except for his hands, which had begun to twitch. Kate wondered if his spirit guide had a drinking problem and, if so, was it Ham-Ata-Arum or Komelecki who experienced the hangover? She bit her lip to stop herself from giggling.

Komelecki went on. "The Creator of All has bestowed free will. It is His gift to us. When children stray into the darkness, someone must lead them out."

"And you're here to do that?" Carl asked sarcastically.

"We bring the message by which you may learn to lead yourselves. That is, Love. God is Love. We are Love. Why wait for the light that encompasses all? It rests within you and leads the way. Nowhere does he go who waits for the journey to take him. There is little to do but travel."

German's head had dropped forward until his head rested on his chest, a trickle of brown liquid running from the corner of his mouth. Every so often he would snort, shift his position, and drift off again. Through it all Komelecki—or Ham-Ata-Arum—continued.

"An entity of consciousness is always aware. Purpose leads. All is known here—heart, soul, mind—where love is. The purpose is search. The purpose brings light. Being and doing are in agreement."

"How do we know you're really a spirit?" Carl challenged.

"Knowing is the sixth sense. Feeling is the seventh. Truth must be known and felt, not sought. Learn to trust, to accept and not flee the truth that surrounds you."

"This has nothing to do with Lynne Hampton," Carl said. "Do you know where she is or don't you?"

Komelecki paused before replying. "Morning must return to the dawn. There are those who wish to know but do not; for in knowing is life, and not all live. Truth stands alone. Reality varies. *Truth*"—he emphasized the word—"never varies. It returns again and again until the thirst is quenched."

"What does that mean?" Brother B. demanded.

"This is not our last parting, for we are here always, holding truth. Remember the light. Love. Love to you all." Komelecki stopped speaking, sat perfectly still for a moment, then collapsed. He almost fell out of the chair, but caught himself at the last possible second.

"Are you all right?" Kate asked him.

Komelecki smiled. "Tired, but well," he replied in a whisper. "You will be pleased to learn that I know where to find Lynne Hampton's body. The session has been a success."

"Then spit it out," Carl demanded. "Or would you rather kill a little more time with your cryptic mumbo jumbo?"

"I shall tell you. Just allow me a moment to recover, please." Komelecki closed his eyes and inhaled deeply. Then, barely audible, he said, "Kate, invite the reporters in."

"You must be nuts," she said without thinking.

"He is," Carl agreed.

"Never mind, Carl," Kate said and sighed. "If they're still there, then let the sharks in. Maybe they've all gone away by now." That was wishful thinking. In fact a few new reporters had arrived, and they were circling on the porch trying to peek through the closed curtains.

Carl hurried to the door and pulled it wide. "Feeding time," he said with a grin. "Open your jaws and come on in."

"You're certainly enjoying yourself," Kate mumbled.

The reporters trampled over each other as they surged through the door. They weren't all legitimate, Kate noticed. Bobby Baxter was editor of the high school paper, which couldn't possibly be interested in this story, but at least Bobby had a legitimate, albeit tenuous, association with journalism. Four or five of the others were just nosy locals. But once inside, everyone with a camera started snapping pictures and firing questions. Komelecki had risen from his chair and was holding his hands up in a request for silence. Surprisingly, he got it.

Kate stumbled through the room turning on lights. Patrick would have a fit if he were here, she thought. Just imagine how this would look to the voting public. Her brother's mayoralty was hanging by a thread.

"Let me explain," Komelecki said. "I have new information concerning Lynne Hampton."

"Is she alive?"

"Where is she?"

"Never mind that. How'd you come by this information?"

Komelecki's calm smile never flickered. "Miss Hampton is no longer on the physical plane. Her spirit, however, cries out to us. Understand that there is no concern for revenge, which in truth is nothing more than a primitive concept of justice. Lynne wishes only to allow her friends and family peace of mind."

"Huh?" German had been wiggling and stretching for a few minutes, but only now did he come fully awake.

"The girl's dead," Carl translated, then turned back to Komelecki. "Where's the body?"

Komelecki gave his beard a few strokes. "The body lies hidden very near here."

"Well, let's go get it!" one of the younger reporters exclaimed, and prepared to dash out the door.

"Please wait," Komelecki said. "Tomorrow I will recover the body. I will leave here at exactly seven-thirteen A.M. Those of you who wish to do so may accompany me."

"That's a weird time," Kate muttered.

Komelecki reached out and patted her arm. "Timing is everything," he said mysteriously.

"Well, I guess the show's over." German pushed himself out of the chair and flexed a few muscles. "Guess I'll be going. And Komelecki, you better stop by the PD and get me tomorrow before you take off on some wild goose chase."

"Take these troublemakers with you, German," Kate pleaded.

"Sure thing, Katie. C'mon, boys."

The reporters argued halfheartedly until one of them finally said, "Hell, Komelecki's not giving us anything until tomorrow. Let's go get a beer."

"Good idea," Kate said. "The Drink Tank is just down the road."

"I'll lead y'all to it," German said cheerfully. "The waitresses are ugly as sin, but at least it's dark."

The reporters followed him happily, and as they stepped off the porch Kate heard German begin one of his let-me-tell-you-about-the-master-criminal-I-almost-captured stories.

Brother B. and his scowling wife were watching Kate, he with a half smile.

"Now that wasn't so excruciating, was it?" Kate asked.

Brother B. reflected for a moment before answering. "A lot of nonsense, if you ask me. None of it made a lick of sense. I can only pray that you have not unleashed the demons of hell upon us."

"But Komelecki says his spirits come from God," Kate argued. "And I haven't seen anything demonic about him, have you?"

"Satan is an expert deceiver. The reverend and I shall pray for you." Mrs. Bradford grabbed her husband's arm and pulled him out the door. "Let's go."

"Hope to see you in church," Brother B. called over his shoulder.

Carl turned to Komelecki. "I'll say this: your concentration is good. That cop's snoring didn't even faze you."

"Actually, when I serve as channel for the spirits, I am not in the room. My own soul goes . . . elsewhere."

"Give it a rest, Komelecki. The suckers are gone."

Komelecki's control was impressive. Carl had been goading him ever since they'd arrived, yet none of the insults had ruffled the psychic. Now, though, Komelecki's unflustered demeanor seemed more the result of preoccupation than mystic tolerance.

"I don't know about the rest of you," Roger said, rising and stretching, "but I had a ball! You know, Kate, you should add this as part of a regular program of entertainment. Picture it: 'Twin Elms Inn presents an assortment of paranormal events for your enjoyment.' You could charge admission, maybe get a few magazines to cover it. . . ."

"I don't believe we've been properly introduced," Komelecki said, and turned to Roger with hand extended.

"What? Oh, by damn, we haven't." Roger shook hands, with enough enthusiasm that Kate was almost convinced of his sincerity. "Roger Shelton. Say, how long have you been selling snake oil? You're awfully good at it."

"Roger, don't you need to put those cars back in your room?" Kate asked quickly.

"Those can wait. I'm interested in talking to Mr. Komelecki here." Roger threw one arm around Komelecki's shoulders and winked at Kate.

"I'd truly enjoy a chat," Komelecki said, suddenly thrown off guard by Roger's chumminess, "but I need some air. It helps to revive me. After communing with the spirits of the night, I always feel the need to rebalance my *chakras*. If you could arrange it, Kate, I'd appreciate absolute quiet when I return." He started out the door before Kate could bid him good night.

"Wait up, Komelecki!" Roger called, and bounded out the door in pursuit. "I'll walk with you."

Kate was concerned. No matter how slick Komelecki might be, she suspected Roger could still outmaneuver him. "Poor man," she said, closing the door behind them.

"Wouldn't it be funny," Carl said, with the same stupid smirk on his face, "if they arrested him for murder?"

"That's dumb. Komelecki wasn't even here when Lynne disappeared."

"I was thinking of that Shelton fellow, actually," Carl said. With that conversation-stopper he headed up the wide staircase, presumably ready for a good night's sleep.

But Carl's suggestion quickly took hold. Suddenly Kate's imagination was painting vivid pictures of Lynne Hampton's body. Komelecki had said it was "hidden very near here." That led Kate to wonder, logically enough, who had hidden it. While a few people had hinted at what reporters liked to call *foul play*, the general assumption had been that Lynne had wandered off alone and was still traipsing through the woods around Jesus Creek. But if Komelecki was right, someone had hidden the girl's body. Meaning someone had killed Lynne—else there wouldn't be a body, would there?

Kate stepped away from the door and wrapped her arms around herself. The sudden silence was disturbing. Funny. She'd evidently grown accustomed to babbling reporters and the constant comings and goings of guests and those blasted children's tortured rendition of the Scriptures. Now the stillness seemed unnatural. She shook her head and began turning off lights, then changed her mind. It wouldn't hurt to leave a few lamps on, she decided. Besides, Komelecki and Roger would be back soon. She might as well tidy up the study while she waited for them.

When Roger and Komelecki hadn't returned by midnight, Kate went to bed. She didn't like leaving the inn unlocked, but it was that or stumble back downstairs later to let them in.

Upstairs, she crawled under the sheets and propped up on a couple of fluffy pillows to read *Slicing Life for a Bigger Serving*. Goodness knows, she thought, I need a bigger serving. I need *a life*.

The dream started before she'd even realized she was asleep. There was a masquerade ball, and Kate, dressed as a slave girl, was trying to dance with some faceless man in a Prince Charming costume. Carl was there, wearing a trench coat. German, too, in a Lone Ranger costume. All together it seemed as if everyone she'd ever known was there, attired in some outlandish costume, and they all kept flitting between her and the prince. But when the clock struck not midnight, but three, and all the guests removed their masks, Kate couldn't take hers off.

She struggled, tugging and clawing at the stupid mask until she broke a sweat. She woke, gasping, and realized she actually was sweating. Why is it so hot in here? she wondered, throwing back the covers.

Tiptoeing out to the hall, she checked the thermostat for the air-conditioning system. It was set to seventy-five degrees, but the thermometer below it registered eighty-five. Kate wiggled the dial and waited to hear the click of the compressor. Nothing.

"Damn," she whispered, and pounded the thermostat with her fist. That didn't help either. If she remembered correctly, the warranty on the unit had run out about two weeks ago. Patrick was going to love this turn of events.

She went back to bed, but tossed and turned without sleeping. She didn't want to chance that nightmare again, anyway. Finally she gave up, pulled a robe over her gown, and went down to the kitchen.

The digital clock said four forty-five. Fifteen minutes before Mrs. Bradford would arrive. No time for a decent breakfast, she decided, so she poured herself a bowl of Frosted Flakes and took it to the window table to watch morning roll in. Sunrise, she told herself, is highly overrated.

By five-fifteen she'd finished eating and cleaning up. Just in time, too. Mrs. Bradford let herself in the back door as Kate was putting away her bowl.

"Hi there," Kate mumbled, feeling as if she were guilty of trespassing. "I couldn't sleep. The air conditioner's on the blink. So I just went ahead and had breakfast. But I cleaned up."

On a good day Mrs. Bradford was intimidating. This morning she reminded Kate of a Stephen King character. Her face was puffy and her eyes bloodshot. Looks like the séance didn't improve her disposition, Kate decided.

Mrs. Bradford did not wish Kate a good morning. She did, however, apologize for her tardiness. "The reverend usually drives me to work, but he was just exhausted this morning, so I made him stay in bed and sleep. He works himself to death, always helping others. Ministering to the sick, tending to the weary in spirit. Always somebody needing him."

"Yes, I expect so," Kate said. "And he deserves to sleep once in a while. I guess you're pretty worn out, too—working here and then discharging all your church duties. And the reenactment. How's that going?"

Mrs. Bradford was single-handedly staging the reenactment of the founding of Jesus Creek, the performance to take place as part of the opening ceremonies of the Sesquicentennial.

"The costumes are almost finished," Mrs. Bradford said. She set her purse on a cabinet shelf and tied an apron around her bulky waist. "So that's not so much trouble now, but the people who are supposed to play the settlers aren't helping any. They don't show up for rehearsal half the time, and when they do they can't remember what they're supposed to do."

"You're making costumes, too? Every time I go

near a sewing machine it starts to make funny noises and jumps around."

"I make all my own clothes," Mrs. Bradford said proudly. "No sense in paying outlandish prices for something I can do myself."

"I agree completely," Kate said, and looked more closely at the dress Mrs. Bradford was wearing. It didn't appear homemade, but it wasn't especially attractive either. "Well, I suppose I'd better get dressed. I'll give J.C. a call about the air conditioner this morning. In the meantime why don't you serve cold cereal this morning? I don't think the guests will mind."

"I was going to make eggs Florentine." Mrs. Bradford already had a cookbook open to the section on eggs.

"Maybe you should wait and see if anyone orders them. The heat may ruin everyone's appetite anyway." Kate left the kitchen grateful that she'd already eaten. Most of the time she felt obligated to try Mrs. Bradford's culinary experiments.

After a long cool shower she dressed in shorts. Patrick wouldn't have approved. He wanted her to dress appropriately for the position, whatever that meant. She brushed her teeth and brushed her hair. She read a few more chapters of *Slicing Life*. She looked out the window and wondered if Lynne's lifeless body was really out there somewhere—and hoped it wasn't. By six-thirty she'd run out of ways to kill time and decided another few minutes of staring out the window would drive her to some drastic act of violence, possibly against herself. Reluctantly, she headed downstairs to face what was certain to be another miserable day.

Carl was there ahead of her. He had shaved and dressed and, for the first time since he'd arrived, around his neck he was wearing a camera— a Kodak VR35.

"Going hiking with the Boy Scouts?" Kate asked.

"You don't think I'd miss this? Say, is it especially hot in here?"

Kate nodded. "The air's conked out. As soon as it's a reasonable hour, I'll phone the repairman."

"Can't you call an emergency number?"

"J.C., our repairman, doesn't answer his home phone. He keeps the machine on to screen his calls. Doesn't like to be disturbed when he's off duty."

Carl shook his head in disbelief. "You mean there's only one guy in this whole town who can fix your air conditioner?"

"Why, no. There are a couple of others. But J.C. is the one we've always used. He'd be offended if we called someone else."

Carl rolled his eyes. "Get me back to civilization," he pleaded.

"Oh, go eat breakfast and shut up. Come on. I'll have coffee with you." Kate led him into the dining room and called for Mrs. Bradford to take the order.

Thank goodness Patrick would be home in a few hours. With luck he'd arrive before Komelecki returned from the search. And then Patrick could deal with whatever commotion ensued.

"What do you think he'll find?" she asked Carl.

"Komelecki? Nothing." Carl was certainly confident this morning. "He'd have done well to say the spirits were out to lunch. How are the scrambled eggs?"

Kate would have warned him but Mrs. Bradford came in just then, prepared to serve coffee immediately. This cardinal rule of waitressing was the only one she'd managed to grasp. "The special this morning is eggs Florentine," she said. "Try it."

"Uh, sure. I'll have that." Carl folded the menu and placed it across the table. "Are you having the same?"

Kate shook her head. "I've already eaten. I'll just have coffee."

Mrs. Bradford rushed back to the kitchen, obviously pleased with this opportunity to try out her newfound recipe.

"What are your plans while we're out digging up bodies?" Carl asked.

In spite of the heat Kate felt a shiver. "You ghoul! Have some respect for that poor girl."

"Who?" Carl asked, genuinely puzzled. "Oh, Lynne Hampton? Didn't it occur to you that, if she is dead, there's bound to be a body to drag back?"

"Do you have to be so morbid?"

Carl shook his head. "What do you mean?"

"Never mind. You asked about my morning. I plan to relax. Once Patrick gets here I may take a vacation."

"Ah, yes. The mayor. What is he, your relief or something?"

"He's the manager of Twin Elms," Kate explained. "I'm just the receptionist slash bookkeeper. Except that I don't really know much about keeping books."

"Then why does your brother keep you on? I'd fire you in a minute and hire someone who was capable." Carl sipped his coffee, as if unaware of Kate's glare.

They sat silently for a few minutes, Carl fantasizing about the pictures he'd be taking and Kate hoping that he'd forget to load the film.

Mrs. Bradford delivered breakfast without comment. Kate watched her as she headed back to the kitchen. The woman moved like a bulldozer, sturdy and solid in the shapeless print dress. But this morning her normal no-nonsense energy seemed to have been diminished. Maybe she, too, was worried about what Komelecki would turn up. Mrs. Bradford hadn't met Lynne—the younger woman had checked in after Mrs. B. had left the inn for the day, and she disappeared that same night—but it was possible that Mrs. Bradford was feeling sympathy for the Hampton family. As far as Kate knew, the Bradfords had no children, but even so it was possible that Mrs. Bradford felt the loss Lynne's parents were suffering.

Looking through the dining room window Kate could see the creek rolling along, and the morning sun hitting the curls of water. There was an old wooden bridge built across it, and just now a couple of schoolboys were leaning against the handrails and throwing stones into the water.

It reminded Kate of a scene from *Tom Sawyer*, except for the fact that these boys were wearing Reeboks and one of them had only a small strip of hair running across his head from front to back. Definitely not from the Christian School. Those students adhered to a strict dress code, and Kate was sure that Mohawk haircuts would not be acceptable to the Bradfords.

The boys on the bridge dug into their backpacks. At first Kate thought they were going to get in a bit of last-minute studying before school, but the books stayed in the packs. Instead each boy sat down on the bridge, legs dangling over the side, and puffed inexpertly on a cigarette. Kate smiled, imagining the conversation that was unfolding out there. They couldn't be more than twelve years old and yet there they were, impressing each other and themselves with this ultimate expression of manhood.

"It's almost time for the show." Carl rose from his chair. "I don't want to miss the grand entrance. Let's wait in the study."

"Sure," Kate agreed. "Why not?" She noticed that Carl had barely touched his breakfast.

Roger was coming down the stairs just as Kate and Carl entered the hallway. He looked as if he'd just climbed out of bed. His eyes were red from lack of sleep, and his chin showed evidence of a reckless shave.

"Rough night, Roger?" Kate asked.

"Yes," he said mournfully. "I'd planned to sleep through the day, but it's started already."

There was no doubt that Roger meant The Reading, which Kate had come to think of as a capitalized horror. "Surely those kids are almost through?"

Roger shook his head. "They're barely into the New Testament. It wouldn't be so bad if that damned PA system didn't squawk—or if the brats could at least enunciate."

"Or if they had a remedial reading teacher," Kate added. "Are you going out there?"

"From the frying pan into the fire," Roger explained. "The library. But first I'll fortify myself with some breakfast from Eloise's."

Kate sighed in sympathy. Estelle Carhart, the librarian, was a class-one airhead. Every time Roger ventured into the Jesus Creek Public Library he returned to the inn sputtering and swearing from frustration.

"Can't be helped," he said. "They've ordered some books for me, and I can't bribe anyone else to pick them up. I'm hoping the assistant librarian will be there rather than Estelle, but my luck has never been particularly good."

"Be brave," Kate told him.

When Roger opened the front door and stepped out onto the porch, Kate could see a good hundred people stomping around on the lawn. Since the students' oral reading was under way, she knew it must be past seven. Seven-ten, the clock in the study told her. "Might as well let them in," she said to Carl. "As my momma always said, 'Ignoring trouble won't make it go away.' "

Carl was loading his camera and didn't even look up, just reached out and pulled the door open. Those in front didn't burst in, as Kate had expected, but filed in quietly, almost reverently. They arranged themselves in neat clusters around the lobby and checked their watches.

Finally someone said, "It's seven-thirteen. Aren't we supposed to leave now?"

No one answered. Kate wasn't about to concur. Besides, it was Komelecki's show, and he probably believed in being fashionably late.

She began to count heads: twenty-two, twenty-three, twenty-*four* reporters—or locals hoping to be mistaken for reporters—plus Carl and his handy camera. Kate realized with a jolt that she was beginning to feel comfortable with these people.

"It's eighteen after. Where's Komelecki?"

"He probably overslept," Kate said. "I'll go up and check on him." She was grateful for the diversion. The intense expectation in there was beginning to make her edgy. She'd been as tense as the others, she had to admit. Not that she believed this psychic foolishness for a minute, mind you. But Komelecki did seem awfully cocksure.

"Stay in the hall," Carl warned with a leer. "No telling what goes on in that room."

"Watch the desk," she snapped, and jogged up the stairs.

Damn Komelecki. He'd upset her cook, disrupted her inn, organized this ghoulish search, and now he'd failed to show up for his own party.

She pounded angrily on Komelecki's door. When she didn't get an immediate response she pounded again. Still no answer. What the hell was he doing—calling up his spirit guide for a map?

Normally Kate had great respect for others' privacy, but nothing about the past few days had been normal. She tried the door, found it unlocked, and stuck her head in the room. Komelecki, of course, wasn't there, and Kate thought it strange that he'd go off and leave the door unlocked like that. But then, maybe he had cast a spell to keep people out of his room. She decided not to test that theory by walking in. He obviously wasn't there, unless he was hiding in the armoire—ridiculous but possible. Still, if he'd chickened out and decided not to face that crowd downstairs, she wasn't cruel enough to give him away.

She tried the bathroom at the end of the hall. No one there, either.

"You'd better tell Mr. Wizard to get his ass down there!" Carl had come bounding up the stairs just as Kate had started down. "The natives are getting restless. Talking about sacrificing a virgin. By the way, would that worry you?"

"He's not here," she said.

"Where is he?"

"How should I know? I checked everywhere up here, and there's no Komelecki. Maybe he left early and plans to make a triumphant return with ..."

"You'd better invent a sharper story than that. I don't think those jokers downstairs are in a congenial mood this morning."

Kate groaned and wiped beads of sweat from her upper lip. "Come on," she said, and grabbed Carl's arm. "I want a bodyguard."

"Aha! You *are* worried about that virgin sacrifice."

The throng in the lobby watched hopefully as Kate descended the stairs, dragging Carl with her. The reporters and an equal number of curiosity-seekers were huddled in the middle of the room, but one stocky fellow by the desk looked up at her and smiled. Kate didn't recognize him, and quickly concluded that he must be an unexpected guest or a salesman. He was slightly bald on top, with a droopy mustache and a bit of belly, but he looked friendly. Right now that counted for a lot, and Kate decided to buy whatever he was selling.

"I'm Kate Yancy," she said, walking behind the desk. "Can I help you with anything?"

He grinned sheepishly, and Kate noticed his dimples. "I know you weren't expecting me. I'm sorry I didn't make a reservation."

"That's no problem," she assured him. "We have a room available. Just sign the register please, and I'll need your license number, too."

"I'm always puzzled by that request. You know, it's not as if anyone ever goes out to my car to see if I lied."

"I'd explain, except I've never figured it out myself. How long do you plan to be with us?"

"Oh, as long as it takes." He scribbled in his name and took the key she offered him.

"The room is upstairs, last door on the left. Just let me know if you need anything, Mr. . . . ." Kate squinted at the scrawl on the ledger.

"Sorry," he said. "I flunked penmanship. I'm Owen Komelecki."

CHAPTER

4

THIS TIME SHE NEEDED CARL'S HELP TO clear the lobby. When the crowd of reporters heard the new guest introduce himself, they latched on to heavy furniture and door frames to keep from being ejected. Determined to get an explanation, they all started talking at once, snapping pictures and shouting at the poor man by the desk.

Dèjá vu, Kate thought. She giggled. The heat was getting to her, no doubt about that.

When the last reporter had been coaxed out with the promise of a full explanation later, Carl double-locked the door. Then he spun around to face the balding man at the desk. "Who the hell are you?" he demanded.

"Owen Komelecki," the man said, obviously bewildered. "I know you weren't expecting me but—"

"You can say that again," Kate mumbled.

Carl looked at her. "Did you get his ID?"

"Of course not. I just assumed . . ."

"Would you like to see my driver's license?" the

stocky man asked. He pulled out his wallet and flipped it open. "Library card? Triple A? No, that's expired."

"Not you," Carl said impatiently. "The other one."

"There are two of me?"

"God forbid. Are there?" Even as Kate said it, it occurred to her that they were getting nowhere.

"Let's start at the beginning," Carl suggested. "Both of you, sit." They did, and Carl started interrogating the new Komelecki. "Now, look. You were expected here two days ago."

Komelecki sat on the edge of his chair and nodded vigorously. "I was, yes. But then the Hamptons canceled the job."

"They what?"

"Canceled. Didn't say why, but that's none of my business, is it? Anyway, this whole incident with the missing girl kept bugging me. I felt I needed to be here. So here I am."

"Okay," Carl said. "Two days ago a man claiming to be Owen Komelecki checked in here. If he's not you, who is he?"

Komelecki shrugged. "Maybe we could ask him."

Kate shook her head. "That's just it. He was supposed to lead that bunch"—she pointed to the mob peering in the window—"on a search for Lynne Hampton's body this morning. Only he's not here. We don't know where he is, and if he's not you then who is he, and why does he use your name, and where is Lynne?"

"He probably heard the real Komelecki was on the way and decided to clear out," Carl suggested.

"No one knew I was coming. I haven't even told my assistant yet. I'll have to give her a call later."

"Maybe he had a vision," Kate said, and giggled again.

Carl glared at her. "Let's take a look in his room. See if he left anything behind."

"But that's invasion of privacy."

"Listen, if this imposter is impersonating me, he deserves to be invaded. Besides, the room's registered in my name, isn't it?"

"Only if you really are Komelecki," Carl reminded him. "But your word will do for now. Let's go."

They made it up the stairs in record time, Carl in the lead. As acting manager of the inn Kate was the one to open the door and enter first, but only because she was able to push Carl out of the way.

Komelecki's room was spick-and-span, even though Glenda hadn't started her rounds yet. The canopied bed was made; Kate couldn't tell whether Komelecki Number One hadn't slept there at all or if he'd made the bed himself. Some guests were excessively tidy. Those were Glenda's favorites.

The room held an armoire, a rolltop desk, a Windsor chair, and a wing chair. Apparently Komelecki had moved in for a lengthy stay. At least he hadn't left his suitcases open on the floor, the way some overnighters did. There was a neatly stacked pile of papers on the desk and a carefully aligned row of pens, pencils, and paper clips. Kate was almost surprised when she didn't see a crystal ball, but she supposed that wasn't an object one left lying around for the maid to fiddle with.

Carl went directly to the desk in the far corner of the room. The new Komelecki followed him. Stifling her principles, Kate peeked inside the armoire. She was almost surprised when she didn't find the false Komelecki cowering inside it.

"His clothes are still here," she announced, pointing to a row of flowing silk shirts. "What do you make of that?"

"He joined a nudist colony?" Komelecki suggested.

"Look at this." Carl was shuffling through a stack of papers on the desk. "Little black book." He started thumbing through it.

Kate snatched the book from Carl's hand. "That's personal. Stop snooping, and see if you can find anything that tells us where he might be."

"Newspaper clippings." Carl had not tried to retrieve the address book but was going through the other papers on the desk. "Chronicling the success of one Owen Komelecki." He held out one clipping to Kate. There was a picture of Komelecki above the story of some mystery he'd solved. It showed a tall, stocky man with a pot belly and a drooping mustache.

"Well, at least we know who you are," Kate said, passing it along to her new guest.

Carl was quickly scanning the press clippings and passing them on to the others. "Here's one about Lynne's stint in the booby hatch. And here's the one I told you about: HAUNTED HOTEL."

Kate snatched that one away from him. "Let me

see that." She read the article quickly. It started with the events surrounding Lynne's disappearance and then reminded the reader that Twin Elms was the site of another mystery.

"Anne McCullough, owner of Twin Elms, died two years ago while the inn was still being renovated. Her body was discovered just outside the inn after dark. Mrs. McCullough died from a gunshot wound to the head. While the young woman lay dying, guests inside the house were celebrating her husband's recent mayoral victory."

"Trash," Kate said. "They're implying that Anne's death and Lynne's disappearance are related."

"Who's Anne?" Komelecki asked.

"She was my brother's wife. She died a couple of years ago, here at the inn. It was her idea to renovate this old dump and turn it into a bed and breakfast. And there's nothing mysterious about the way she died—it was suicide. Although good luck getting this scandal sheet to print a retraction."

"There was no question about the cause of death, then?" Komelecki asked.

"None at all. The inn was full of people attending Patrick's victory party, and we all heard the shot." Kate didn't add that she had been the first out the door to investigate; nor did she mention that she had found Anne just seconds before her sister-in-law died. The nightmares had haunted her for months afterward, and she didn't want to resurrect them.

Carl didn't seem to be listening. "More on Lynne," he said. "Boy, this guy really reads up on his subject. He's done almost as much homework as I have."

"Maybe that's how psychics work," Kate suggested.

"No," Komelecki told her. "Normally it's best to avoid information on the subject. Less interference. Less chance of getting thrown off the scent, you know."

"The Psychic Times." Kate picked up one of several magazines that had been stacked on the desk. "What's that?"

"New Age rag," Komelecki said. "Articles about ancient vibrations and filtered cerean harmonics. If you look in the back, there's probably an ad for a degree in Psychic Prediction or some such. Just mail in your check or money order today."

"Sounds like our man," Kate admitted. "Is there anything in there about séances?"

"Séances?" Komelecki grinned.

"Trance-channeling," Carl corrected. "How many times do I have to tell you? It's trance-channeling."

"You're kidding." Komelecki's grin widened. "Did this guy summon up the spirits?"

"Yeah. Don't you?" Carl asked with a little sneer.

"Only from a bottle." Komelecki was absent-mindedly flipping through one of the magazines. "I think you'd better call the police. See if they can locate this man."

Carl cocked his head to one side and folded his arms across his chest. "Can't you find him? Any psychic worth his salt should be able to do that."

"Why bother?" Kate said, pointing to the closet

full of clothes. "He's bound to come back pretty soon."

"Are you kidding? By now the whole town knows the real Komelecki is here. The other guy is about a hundred miles away."

Carl made sense.

"Okay," Kate agreed reluctantly. "I'll call the cops. But you know who'll show up."

"Yeah," Carl said, and Kate could have sworn she saw a sadistic gleam in his eye.

Downstairs Kate dialed the number for the PD, as German liked to call it. An eight-by-ten-foot room below the tax assessor's office hardly deserves a title, she thought, but she supposed it made German feel like a real cop. Lord, she'd be glad when the chief got back to town. Reb Gassler might have his flaws, but at least he wasn't addicted to chewing tobacco.

As she waited for an answer—four rings . . . five rings . . . thank goodness this wasn't an emergency—she heard Komelecki ask Carl about food.

"They've got a great breakfast here," Carl said, with a sideways glance at Kate. "Try the eggs Florentine."

"What's up?" German helped himself to a wing chair and propped his feet on the mahogany coffee table. Kate wondered if pointy-toe cowboy boots were part of his regulation uniform.

German carried that oversized gun on his hip, but he'd probably never fired it except at an occasional tin can, Kate figured. And she doubted if he could hit that. She didn't think for a minute that the man was a suitable cop, but with only four men on the force there wasn't much to choose from. The truly frightening thing was that, when Reb Gassler retired, by right of seniority German would be next in line for the position. And barring a major disagreement with the mayor, he could expect to hold the job for life. No wonder he was so confident.

Kate sighed and sat down on the love seat facing him. "German, have you seen Komelecki this morning?"

"Nope. He was supposed to come by the PD before he took off on his search, but I ain't seen him yet."

"He's disappeared. That's why you *ain't* seen him."

"No kidding! He does magic tricks, too, huh?"

Kate took a deep breath and counted to ten. This was going to be worse than she'd imagined. "No, German. He's gone from the inn. And probably from town, too."

"So? Reckon he's free to do that."

"But his clothes are still here."

German shrugged and moved a lump from one cheek to the other. "Maybe he's gained weight."

"The thing is, he's not really Komelecki."

"Who is he?"

"I don't know."

German put his feet on the floor and leaned slowly forward. "Then how do you know he's not Komelecki?"

Kate was sweating now, not to mention irritable from lack of sleep. She fought an impulse to scream.

"Because the real Komelecki is in the dining room right now."

"How do you know he's the real one?"

"I saw his driver's license and library card, German. Now pay attention. You have to find the phony Komelecki. Put out an ABP or whatever you call it."

"APB. Why?"

"Why? Because he's impersonating a psychic. There must be a law against that."

"Not that I know of." German mulled it over for a minute. "Did he happen to con anybody out of their money?"

"Well, how about the Hamptons? They're paying his expenses here, and I guess some sort of fee."

"They hired him, right? It's up to them to make sure he's the real thing. People believe in all sorts of nonsense. Look at them TV preachers."

"This is different, German. The real Komelecki said the Hamptons changed their minds about him coming here."

"So? That doesn't stop them from hiring this other guy, does it? Besides, how do you know he's not a real psychic? Just because he's using the other guy's name?"

"Of course he's phony. And why would they hire one psychic then fire him just to hire another one, phony or not?"

German shrugged. "What's the difference? A psychic's a psychic."

"Damn it, German!" Kate had come to the end of her considerable patience. "Go find this guy. Put him in jail and keep him there until we figure out what he's done."

"Now, Katie. You've got it backwards. First he's got to break the law, and then we arrest him."

Well, there it was: German Hunt, of all people, was more rational than she was. What a frightening concept. Kate closed her eyes and took a deep breath while counting to ten.

"Fine," she said at last, struggling to keep her voice under control. "But will you at least keep an eye out for him? And let us know if you see him?"

"Oh, I guess I could do that. When did you last see him?"

"Last night, just after the séance. He followed you out."

"Which way did he go?"

Kate shook her head. "I have no idea."

"Uh-huh," German said and rose slowly from his chair. "Well, I'll see what I can do. But to tell you the truth, Katie, I don't imagine this guy'll be back."

Kate closed the door behind German and leaned against it, fighting the urge to pound her head against the nearest wall. Those reporters were still out there, revived by this new mystery. No doubt German would spend the next hour or so regaling them with sagas from his exciting career. Serves them right, Kate thought viciously, then chided herself for that ungracious attitude. Lately it had occurred to her that she might not be cut out for a job that put her in constant contact with the public.

* * *

"German can't help," Kate said, entering the dining room. "Unless Komelecki actually commits a crime. Or unless German runs over him with the patrol car."

"We might file a missing persons report if he doesn't show up soon," Komelecki said.

Carl pushed his chair back and stood up. "You do as you please. I'm going to track down Komelecki. There's got to be a great story in this."

"I sure hope you find him," Kate said.

The real Komelecki shook his head sadly. "I hope you find another name for him. This is ridiculous."

"Actually I can think of several," Carl said brightly.

"Oh, get lost, Carl." Kate rolled her eyes. She was in no mood to tolerate him today.

"You'll miss me," he said, blowing her a kiss as he left the room.

Kate took his empty chair and studied Komelecki for an instant. He doesn't look like a man with supernatural powers, she thought. If you put him on a crowded street no one would even notice him, except for that little dribble of egg on his shirt. "Mr. Komelecki," she said, "I'm sorry about this confusion. I know it must be frustrating. Is there any way I can make amends?"

"Yes," he said sincerely. "Eat the rest of these eggs."

Kate nodded sympathetically. "Don't worry. I'll treat you to real food later." And that reminded her: If one psychic upset Mrs. Bradford, imagine what two would do. "Did our cook happen to catch your name?"

"As a matter of fact, Carl introduced us."

"Oh, dear. How did she take it?"

"She seemed to take an immediate dislike to me. Am I being overly sensitive?" He speared a morsel of egg with his fork but hesitated about putting it in his mouth.

"No. Mrs. Bradford is . . . a little neurotic."

"You don't think she could be a poisoner?" He set the fork down, egg uneaten.

"Probably not. Not on purpose anyway, but she may try to save your soul. Watch out for fire and brimstone."

Komelecki raised his eyebrows. "Is that what she puts in the food?"

Kate shook her head. "I don't think so. Her husband's a preacher. He gets most of his inspiration from her."

"Probably gas."

"She's fervently opposed to psychics. You should've been here the other night. They brought their entire congregation along for choir practice on our front lawn. And they tried to run . . . your predecessor out of town." Kate thought for a moment. "I suppose we should consider that, shouldn't we? I mean, maybe they scared him off. Of course, it hasn't done them any good, because he wasn't even you, and now you're here anyway."

Komelecki pulled out a handkerchief and wiped his forehead. "How do I get myself into these messes?"

"Goes with the job, I expect. But I'm glad you're not like the other one."

"Oh? And what is he like?"

"You know," Kate said, trying to think of a polite way to phrase it. "He's sort of colorful."

Komelecki nodded. "I hear most psychics *are* colorful. That's probably why no one ever recognizes me. I don't fit the part."

Glenda breezed through the kitchen just then. "Sorry to be late," she said. "Overslept."

"Our maid," Kate explained, as Glenda disappeared. "But only part-time. Really she's a beauty queen."

"Interesting household you've got here. Any other members I should be warned about?"

"Just my brother, who'll be here any time. And me, of course. At the moment we have one other guest, not counting Carl. Roger's pretty much living here until he finds a place of his own. Roger Shelton. He collects model cars, then puts motors in them and races them on a little track."

"Slot cars," Komelecki said. "I thought that was a dead hobby."

"Excuse me," Glenda said, poking her head back around the door. "That's Patrick on the phone. He wants to talk to you, Kate."

"No," Kate said. "No, no, no."

"I can tell him you're busy," Glenda suggested.

"No, that's okay, Glen. But I can tell you exactly what he's going to say." She excused herself and crossed the dining room and hallway to the study.

Picking up the receiver, she began with, "Absolutely not, Patrick. You're not going to do this to me again."

"Don't get excited, Katherine. I just wanted you to know I'll be a little later than I anticipated."

"How late?" she demanded.

"I should be there by Sunday."

"*What?* But that's when the celebration starts! You're the mayor, for Pete's sake! What if your plane's late? What if . . . ?"

"German can fill in for me. I've already called Sheila, so don't worry about that. How's everything there?"

"Just peachy," Kate told him. "We've got *two* psychics—but one is missing, and Mrs. Bradford is trying to poison the other. Reporters are giving birth in the yard, illiterate children are babbling into that damned PA system you donated, the air conditioner is dead, and I have an auction to put together sometime before my next scheduled nervous breakdown."

"I can tell you've got it all in hand," he said absently. "See you Sunday."

Kate heard the click before she could respond. "Damn!" she cried, slamming the receiver onto the cradle. Turning, she saw that Komelecki had followed her into the study.

"I think I'll unpack now," he said quietly.

"Need help?" It was a stupid question, but the smart ones eluded her for the moment.

"Oh, no," he assured her. "You seem to have your hands full as it is."

Kate nodded and bit her lip. "I've had better days." Her voice was dangerously high-pitched.

"Anything I can do?"

Kate took a deep breath and tried to smile. "Can you blow up that sound system?"

Komelecki tilted his head to one side. "I've been meaning to ask. What is that?"

"The Traditional Faith Church's contribution to our Sesquicentennial celebration. The kids are reading the entire Bible."

"Twenty-four hours a day?"

"No, it just seems that way. They read from seven to five. They're supposed to be finished sometime Sunday, presumably before the official festivities begin."

Komelecki perked up instantly. "Sunday? Gives us a reason for living, doesn't it?"

"You don't ask for much."

"Just give me time to warm up." He picked up the suitcase he'd left by the desk.

"Speaking of warming up, the repairman will be here anytime to fix the air conditioner. I hope you won't be too uncomfortable in the meantime."

"Oh." Komelecki seemed pleasantly surprised. "It's broken? I thought maybe you were striving for atmosphere. Guess I can stop worrying about the outdoor john."

With Patrick away, and the faulty air conditioning, and the dual Komeleckis to deal with, Kate had fallen behind on the auction. She still had late donations to pick up, then everything had to be tagged, listed on three different forms, and priced appropriately, so the auctioneer would have an idea of starting bids. There was no choice now but to spend the entire day finishing the job.

The combination of the heat and the droning children's voices had made local merchants irritable,

she noticed. Even sweet old Mr. Pate at the hardware store had snapped at her. And she thought
he'd probably only given her half the merchandise
he'd originally intended to donate. Well, it wasn't
her fault, was it? He could blame Patrick for that
damned PA nuisance.

She left the hardware store in a foul mood, cursing under her breath at no one in particular. Miss
Constance Winter, the town loony, had met her just
outside and forced a coconut brownie into her hand.
"Eat it in good health, dearie," the old woman com-
manded.

It wasn't that Kate didn't adore Miss Constance.
But she was wearing a beret and a plaid wool coat,
and just thinking about it in this heat was enough
to make Kate swoon. As she ambled away, Miss
Constance broke into song.

One of those little cars, the kind that resembles
a squashed bug, whizzed by and narrowly missed
hitting Kate when she stepped off the curb; then
the driver had the nerve to flash her an obscene
gesture. But the last straw was the parking ticket
on the van's windshield. Didn't German have anything better to do? No, German wouldn't be passing
out parking tickets. He must have assigned that
useless task to J.D., the newest officer.

Kate decided to take a lunch break that she didn't
have time for. Eloise's was empty except for Benny
and Chester, who occupied their regular table by
the door. The air conditioner was blowing full blast.
Kate sat on one of the stools at the counter and held
a frosty glass of ice water against her cheek.

"It could be worse," Eloise said.

"Really?" Kate asked. "How?"

"For one thing you could be running the beauty pageant instead of the auction. Imagine having to deal with beautiful, brain-dead girls all day."

"Frankly, I don't know why they enter. Glenda's going to win."

"I said they were brain-dead, didn't I?" Eloise set a glass of iced tea in front of Kate. "How's the auction?" She propped her elbows on the counter.

"I'm almost finished, I think. Unless I've forgotten something vital, and I probably have. I owe you my life. If you hadn't helped me collect the items . . ."

"No problem. But since you brought it up"—Eloise leaned across the counter—"you could do me a favor. Set me up with that cute reporter."

"Carl?" Funny, Kate wouldn't have figured him for Eloise's type.

Eloise nodded. "Honey, if you're not making use of him, I might as well. No sense letting him go to waste."

"For you, anything. If I ever see him again I'll hand over his leash."

"He's gone?" Eloise seemed to be on the verge of a pout.

"No, no," Kate assured her. "He's stalking a Komelecki."

"I hear you've had two of them already. Why's Carl after another one?"

"Not another one. The first one has disappeared. He was supposed to escort a pack of people on a search this morning. Said his spirit guide told him where to find Lynne's body. But he didn't show up.

Then the second Komelecki appeared, and we're pretty sure he's the real thing; presumably the first one wasn't even psychic to start with. I can't believe you haven't heard about this."

"I've been busy with an all-morning rush," Eloise said. "You just managed to miss it. But that first psychic was in here the other day, and if that's his normal behavior, I'd say you're lucky he's gone."

"Why?" Kate asked. "What happened?"

Eloise chuckled a little to herself. "First he ordered a salad, right? With lemon juice, not salad dressing. And when I brought it out to him, he blessed it."

"You mean he said grace," Kate translated.

"No, I mean he blessed it. Just like the preacher does to the grape juice on sacrament Sunday. Stood up there beside the table, held out his hands, and chanted some kind of poem over the salad."

Kate shook her head, chuckling now herself.

"And the next time he came in he—Say, have you checked with Glenda? She may have stomped your psychic into mush and made bread with him."

"Glenda doesn't have a violent bone in her body."

"You don't get me. She came in here last night, and he was right behind her. They sat over there at that table for a while, and then Glenda left with him. Or he left with her. I think he sort of followed."

"Really?" Kate sipped at her tea and tried to imagine how on earth someone like Komelecki One had convinced someone like Glenda Richmond to spend any time with him at all. "When was this?"

"Just before closing. About eleven, I guess. And

they left together while I was cleaning up for the night."

"That's funny, because when he left the séance Roger was dogging him. You know how Roger likes to bug people."

Eloise nodded. "You had a séance? Good for you, Kate. You're loosening up at last."

"Believe me, it wasn't my idea. Mr. So-Called Komelecki insisted that it was the fastest way to contact the spirits. We held it in the study."

"What did the spirits say? And why wasn't I invited?" Eloise retrieved Kate's lunch from the serving window and placed it in front of her.

"Eloise, if I'd known you were interested I'd gladly have invited you to take my place. You'd have been disappointed, anyway. The spirits weren't very chatty. Probably because Komelecki was a fraud."

"Well now that you've got another one, why not have another séance? And this time don't forget me."

Kate shook her head. "This new guy doesn't handle it that way—he seems almost normal. But I guess anyone would, compared to the last one."

"So what is this new one like? Is he cute?"

"Yeah," Kate said thoughtfully. "He is kind of cute. In a funny sort of way."

A blast of heat at her back made Kate turn. Roger had opened the door and sailed in. He was humming under his breath and smiling broadly.

"Kate, my dear child. And lovely, talented Eloise," he said, pressing both hands to his chest. "What wonderful company. I'm glad I came in."

"I thought you were spending the morning at the library," Kate said. "I've never seen you emerge from a battle with Estelle in quite this mood."

Roger settled on the stool next to her and shrugged. "Estelle was especially diplomatic today. She stayed in the back room most of the time I was there. Even better than that, I met a very interesting woman. Either of you know Delia Cannon? She works at the library part-time."

"Oh, no. Roger, you *didn't* inflict yourself on Delia. Say you didn't." Kate was truly concerned. Delia Cannon was a former elementary school teacher, and easily the most popular person in Jesus Creek. Like Kate, Delia was recently divorced. That, to Kate, meant that she was probably still suffering from the insecurity brought on by the sure knowledge that the failed marriage had been her fault.

"I didn't inflict myself," Roger said. "I was a *gentleman*. Amazing woman. Do you know, she already understands the difference between HO and one twenty-fourth?"

"You made her listen to slot-car talk? Roger, don't do that to Delia. She's nice."

Roger nodded happily. "Of course she is. I just *said* that, didn't I?"

He turned his attention to the menu, while Kate and Eloise watched him with suspicion. Something had gotten into Roger, and neither of them quite knew what.

Kate arrived home long after the Bible-reading had ended for the day. She kicked off her shoes and stretched out across the love seat as best she could, hoping no one would interrupt her moment of self-pity. The one luxury she missed most since coming back to share the inn with Patrick was a private living room.

"There you are." J.C. came through the back hall, wiping his hands on a grease-stained rag. "You got a problem, all right."

Kate groaned and struggled to sit up. "How big a problem?"

"Compressor's shot. Get you a new one, but it'll take a week or so. Get you a whole new unit tomorrow, but that'll cost more." J.C. ran his arm across his sweat-drenched forehead.

Kate wondered how *much* more but didn't ask. "Fine. If you can install it tomorrow, I'll take the whole unit."

"Reckon I ought to talk to your brother about that?"

"Forget my brother," Kate snapped. "If he'd stay around here and run this stupid place . . . Never mind. Just get the new unit installed as soon as you can."

J.C. shrugged. "Tomorrow afternoon then. I'll drive over to Benton Harbor to pick it up in the morning."

Kate sank back onto the sofa as J.C. let himself out the front door. She had a good mind to order all brand-new appliances. And furniture, too. Throw out the antiques and replace them with chrome tables. Take down the heavy velvet drapes and put up Venetian blinds. String multicolored fluorescent lights across the lobby.

Komelecki Two interrupted her plans for redec-
oration. "Is it dinnertime, or do you have another
date?"

Kate groaned again. "I'm sorry. I just can't bring
myself to put those shoes on again. But I'll give you
directions to a restaurant."

"I have an amazingly poor sense of direction.
Why don't I fix something for both of us? Or will
your cook mind?"

"She minds everything," Kate said, and smiled
weakly. "Do you know how to cook?"

"Do I know how to cook? Follow me." Komelecki
led the way through the dining room and into the
kitchen.

"Here. Sit." He pulled a chair out and placed it
so that Kate could lean back and prop her feet on
another chair.

The kitchen had been the last section of the house
to be remodeled, and Kate had insisted on design-
ing it herself. Since she wasn't much of a cook herself she'd relied on magazine articles and advice
from Eloise. But because of her personal involve-
ment, she considered the kitchen her favorite room
in the inn. The counters had been topped with wood
to match the original floor. The windows over the
industrial-size sink had only lace valances at the
top, so that in the morning the sun shone through
them and lit up the kitchen better than any lights
could have done. And in one corner she'd included
a breakfast nook. It was cozy and friendly, but no
one ate breakfast there when Mrs. Bradford was
around.

Kate sat at the small table now and tucked her

skirt between her bare legs. "What are you planning to make?" she asked him.

"I don't know. We'll just have to wait and see what it looks like."

Terrific, Kate thought as she watched him rummage through the fridge. I'm at the mercy of a flying-by-the-seat-of-his-pants cook.

"Do you know," he asked incredulously, "that there is nothing in here but breakfast food?"

"Well, Mrs. Bradford only cooks breakfast. That's why we call this a bed and breakfast inn."

"Don't you eat other meals? You live here, after all." Komelecki threw a package of bacon on the counter.

"I live here. I don't eat here. If you think those eggs were poison, you should try my cooking. Hey, I didn't know you could fix bacon in the microwave."

Komelecki grinned. "You really can't cook, can you?"

"No. So how did you amuse yourself today? Inhaling 'vibrations'?"

He looked puzzled. "Is that a quaint colloquial expression?"

"No, I thought it was a psychic term."

Komelecki's mouth twitched. "I gather you picked it up from my namesake."

Kate nodded. "Is it wrong, or just corny?"

Komelecki, unable to find an appropriate pan, draped bacon strips on a paper towel and put them in the microwave. "Two minute nuke," he said, then turned to Kate. "Nonexistent. But don't let that bother you. Most of these so-called psychic emanations are nonexistent, too. And as for my day, I walked around your lovely town and took pictures."

Funny, he didn't look like the touristy type. "Why?"

"Because," he said, enthusiastically grating cheese, "that's my profession. I'm a photographer. And I don't often get a chance to shoot what I want."

"Somehow photography and psychic detection don't seem to mesh. I mean, psychics are sort of romantic, you know. And I had this art class in high school where we had to make a camera with a shoebox and a bunch of other household stuff. It wasn't the least bit romantic. In fact, I got a D for the term."

"I find that the two mesh quite happily. Portrait photography pays the bills, and having my own business lets me take time off whenever an intriguing case comes along. As for the psychic detection . . . I like to think of myself as a heavyset lens."

"But what about customers? You still have to schedule appointments, don't you?"

He opened a can of pineapple rings before answering. "Yes, but I can reschedule those. I'm the boss. Actually I have my assistant reschedule, so *I* don't get yelled at."

"Your assistant must receive a generous salary."

"No way. That's why assistants are so damned hard to keep. I'm breaking in a new one right now, in fact. I'm always breaking in a new one. Hope she remembers to cancel that sitting tomorrow. Remind me to check."

"Wouldn't you *know*? Can't you just . . . ?" Kate wiggled her fingers and squinted.

"I don't read minds," he said patiently. "I get impressions."

"Do you get the impression, then, that your business is thriving?"

"My business has never thrived." He put crisp bacon strips on an English muffin, smothered it with grated cheese, and topped it off with a pine-apple ring. Then he made a second one, which, Kate surmised, meant that she would have to eat one of the nasty-looking concoctions. " 'Eked out a living' would be the more accurate description."

"Aha. So when do you plan to make your first million?"

Komelecki peeked into the oven and said firmly, "I'm surprised and disappointed. Is affluence a prerequisite for friendship with you?"

"No. That was a joke." Kate shook her head. "Besides, my brother takes care of that for me. The last three guys I went out with were interrogated mercilessly by Patrick, and I never heard from them again."

"Really? You and Patrick must be very close. I always wanted a little sister to take care of."

"We are not close. Patrick just likes to run my life."

"And what does Patrick do when he isn't twisting your arm behind your back?"

Kate was fairly certain she didn't like his implication, but she was too tired to spar. "Patrick owns the inn, he sells insurance, and in his spare time he's mayor of Jesus Creek."

"Respectable jobs, all. And how did you get here?"

"Took a left in Albuquerque." Kate was glad he laughed. Komelecki was the saddest-looking man she'd ever met, despite his cheery face. Or maybe that was resignation she saw in his eyes. In his line of work he'd have to have it or he'd go nuts.

"Are you into politics, too?" he asked.

"God, no!"

"Well, you must have *something* in common with your brother."

"I have nothing in common with any member of my family. I'm a changeling. When I was a kid I went through all my parents' possessions looking for the adoption papers."

"I don't suppose you found them." Komelecki peeked into the oven again.

"Of course not. Although I'm still not convinced." Kate leaned her head back and sighed. "Imagine how disappointed my mother must have been. She probably had dreams of me as a regular little debutante. And look what she got: a woman who doesn't even own a decent pair of panty hose."

Komelecki turned and gave her a serious look. "I'll adopt you, if you'd like."

"Thanks, but I'd be more trouble than I'm worth. Unresolved familial conflicts, according to Dr. Fenton."

"Your shrink?"

"No. Dr. Fenton wrote *Finding Your Place on the Family Stage*. You haven't read it? I could lend it to you."

"Thanks anyway," he said quickly. "I probably

won't have time to read it. I don't expect to be here very long."

"You think you know where Lynne is?" Kate sat up straighter in her chair.

"Not at the moment. But I expect she'll turn up on her own soon." He took the sandwiches out of the oven and started looking for plates.

"You think she's alive then?"

Komelecki shrugged. "I'd say so. I've been wrong before though."

"I hope you're right this time. I only met her once, but I liked her. She reminded me of me, a little. God knows why."

"Because she's innocent and vulnerable?" Komelecki suggested.

"Lynne? Worldly or sophisticated, yes. But innocent and vulnerable?"

"Worldly doesn't mean not hurting. And you're the kind of person who responds to vulnerability in other people. Most of us do. That's why we all like kittens and puppies."

"I know a very nice man who hates kittens," Kate said. "What does that say about him?"

"Definitely a warped personality. No one staying here at the inn, I hope." Owen leaned against the counter to eat, bachelor-style, while she balanced a plate on her lap to avoid having to put her feet down and eat at the table.

Kate took the first bite cautiously. Surprisingly, Owen's strange concoction was tasty. "This is great," she said. "How long are you going to stay?"

"Want to hire me to cook? I guess I'll stay until whenever. Until it's time to go."

"Sounds like the theme song from some old Western," Kate said. "Too bad Carl isn't here to enjoy this."

"He's the one who lured me into those eggs this morning. If he were here, I might have laced his sandwich with something deadly."

"Wow! *You* could. I mean, being psychic and all, you could kill someone and get away with it. You'd know what the cops were going to do before they did it." Kate had gotten so excited she'd almost knocked her plate onto the floor.

"Kate, I've told you. It doesn't work that way. I can't open up a head and see what's inside."

"Too bad. I can think of scads of uses for a talent like that."

Owen winked at her. "I have other methods."

After this dinner and a quick cleanup in the kitchen, Kate felt considerably better. She walked with Owen as far as the entry hall. "Thanks for the sandwich," she told him. "I owe you one."

"You aren't going to cook, are you? If bacon and microwaves are beyond your ken . . ."

"I promise I'll think of some way other than cooking to repay you."

Before she could consider the possible implications of that statement, Carl stormed through the front door. He was sweating seriously. A layer of red dust covered his face.

"What happened to you?" Kate asked.

"That damned cop," Carl snarled.

"German? My, you've changed your opinion about him, haven't you?"

"Hell, no. I never liked the jackass. But he wasn't in my way before."

"What are you babbling about? How is German in your way?"

Carl glared at her, as if it were her fault. "He's got Lynne Hampton, and he won't let me near her."

CHAPTER
5

CARL PACED BACK AND FORTH, FROM THE registration desk on the far side of the study to the door on the other side. As Kate and Owen tried to extract an explanation from him, he continued to question the legitimacy of German's pedigree. "I'd like to rip that badge right off his chest. For that matter, I'd like to rip off his chest."

"Don't be ridiculous—and stop kicking my desk," Kate warned him. "Start at the beginning and tell us what happened. No more of this silly temper tantrum." Carl stopped in the middle of the room, arms held straight against his sides as if trying to contain his anger. Through clenched teeth, he muttered, "When I was at the police station—"

"What were you doing there?" Kate interrupted.

"Trying to find your psychic. Now shut up and let me finish."

"Sorry. Go ahead."

"While I was there a call came in. Somebody had

103

seen a naked woman wandering along the highway
outside of town. So I went along for the ride."

"Naturally," Kate said.

"It sounded like a story, okay? A good reporter
never sleeps. Anyway, I rode out with German. And
there she was, stumbling down the road and singing at the top of her lungs."

Owen was listening intently, but he allowed Kate
to play inquisitor. She didn't mind. It gave her an
opportunity to put Carl on the defensive for a
change.

"How did Lynne look?" Kate asked. "Is she
okay?"

Carl rolled his eyes. "Does she *sound* okay? She
was dirty and stark naked, and she kept babbling
about the Rebirth."

"What about rebirth?"

"She said she'd been waiting for it, or something.
Trying to find it. And she mentioned aliens that
take over human brains."

"Perfectly logical comment from a woman walking naked down the street, I'd say," Owen said.

"But here's the kicker," Carl said, and spun
around to punch the wall. "That son of a bitch
stashed the girl in the patrol car and threw me out."

"What do you mean, threw you out? Bodily?"

"He ordered me out of the car. I had to walk
back." Carl's face turned an exotic shade of purple.
"I've been walking for hours. Not one person even
slowed down. I thought you small-town hicks were
supposed to be friendly."

"Not since television news was introduced. Even
in Jesus Creek we've heard about the dangers of

picking up hitchhikers." Kate looked him over, taking in his dust-covered face, disheveled hair, and sweat-soaked shirt. She doubted he'd have been rescued even by the most trusting soul. "And you couldn't have been walking for *hours*. Jesus Creek isn't that big, even if you took all the side roads. Now, where is Lynne?"

"Hell, I don't know. Hospital, I guess. Where's the nearest one?"

"County Medical Center," Kate told him. "It's a little red-brick building on the corner of Morning Glory Way and Wicken. But I doubt they'll give us any information. You know how hospitals are."

"I'll get information," Carl said firmly.

Kate sat cross-legged in the middle of her bed, wrapped in a faded terry bathrobe and with her wet hair falling on her shoulders. She'd tried to lose herself in *Curing Your Own Insecurities*, but her mind kept wandering away from the convoluted explanation for built-in childhood reactions. Where was the first Owen Komelecki? she wondered. Or perhaps, that K person. Mr. U. N. Owen. She hated to keep calling him Komelecki, after all. And why had he disappeared so suddenly? He couldn't have known the real Owen was about to arrive, yet he'd managed to leave just hours (minutes?) before his cover was blown.

And where had Lynne been all this time? Kate thought the poor girl probably could benefit from some of the self-help books piled up on the dresser and table. Lynne had all the symptoms, and if anyone could recognize them it was Kate.

The only real difference between them was that Kate's parents had been middle class with ambition, whereas Lynne's family had the money and power that Kate's would have killed for. And because of that Lynne had a hard time escaping. Kate had simply married the high school troublemaker and headed off on his Harley to a life of . . . well, not freedom exactly. Freedom implied doing what one wished, and Kate had actually spent years taking unpleasant jobs for minimum wage to support Tony's motorcycle.

But Lynne had nowhere to hide. Her family could always track her down. And would, to save face. It was clear they weren't particularly concerned about Lynne, or someone from the family would have shown up in Jesus Creek. Instead they'd left the job to the local police and finally called in a psychic or two. No wonder Lynne was so screwed up.

Kate finally gave up on the book and threw it aside. Maybe she'd visualize new wallpaper, using the technique Komelecki No. 1 had suggested. The dainty pink rosebuds on her walls had been chosen by Anne, before Kate had arrived. "Will thinking make it so?" she mumbled, and slid back onto her pillow.

Closing her eyes, she whispered *om* a few times and forced her body to relax. Now what would she like to see in her own future? She quickly scanned the likeliest goals—money, fame, happiness—but decided she probably should be more specific. By the time her deepest desire occurred to her she was already drifting into sleep.

* * *

Roger was just finishing the Saturday morning breakfast of croissants (microwaved Sara Lee) with cheese and fruit when Kate staggered into the dining room. "You're up early. And eating Mrs. Bradford's breakfast, too. What's gotten into you?"

Roger pointed to the extra chair at his table and motioned her into it. "I have packing to start this morning. Also, I'm meeting Delia Cannon for a quick tour of historic Jesus Creek."

"Ha!" Kate said cynically. "Since when do you care anything about history?"

"Just between you and me? Since I met the lovely Ms. Cannon."

"She's a darned nice lady," Kate said. "You'd better treat her like one. Otherwise I'll come after you myself with a baseball bat."

Uncharacteristically, Roger didn't respond with one of his unanswerable zingers. Instead he smiled sheepishly. "Yeah," he sighed. "She's nice. Cute, too."

"I don't believe this. You've got a crush on Delia." Kate was genuinely surprised. She hadn't thought Roger capable of sincere emotion.

"Too soon to tell if it's a crush or the real McCoy. But get back to me this evening. I'll know by then." He pushed back his chair and finished the last of his coffee while standing. "I'm off to see the Wizard, the wonderful Wizard of Love," he sang, and exited on a high note.

Owen came in cautiously, as if expecting an attack. "Is that one of your residents?"

"Yes," Kate replied, still stunned by Roger's behavior. "It's the damnedest thing. I think he's falling in love."

"Oh well, that explains it." Owen helped himself to Roger's deserted chair. "I'm glad to see another morning person. Besides Romeo out there."

"No way. I have an auction to arrange, or I'd sleep until noon."

Owen tensed. "Should I go away? Are you grumpy in the morning?"

"No, no," Kate said quickly. "Talk to me and keep me awake. And speaking of morning people, someone from the Hamptons' called at the crack of dawn. Said to tell you 'Thanks, and the check is in the mail.' Much more formal than that of course, but that's the Reader's Digest version."

Owen frowned. "How did they know I was here?"

"Well they hired you, didn't they?"

"They also fired me," he reminded her.

"I'd forgotten. Are you sure you understood them correctly? Are you absolutely positive they called you off the case?"

"Absolutely positive." Owen nodded vigorously. "My assistant took the call and then double-checked. People don't usually cancel. Most of them give serious consideration before they hire a psychic, but once they do they're steadfast."

Kate yawned. "The Hamptons have a reputation for eccentricity. Maybe that's it. They probably heard about you—the other you, that is—being here and decided to let it go. How would they know it wasn't you, after all?"

"Could be," Owen said thoughtfully.

Mrs. Bradford came in then with the coffeepot.

She flinched when she saw Owen, but managed to hold her position to indicate that she was ready to take his breakfast order.

"Just cereal," he told her quickly. "Anything that doesn't have oat bran or fiber."

Mrs. Bradford didn't reply, but from the way she stomped back into the kitchen, with squared shoulders and something like a muttered grunt, Kate assumed she'd heard.

"You'll be sorry," Kate told him. "She waters down the milk. We can't get her to stop. She's convinced she's protecting us from bankruptcy. Mrs. Bradford is extremely thrifty."

"This is a very strange place," Owen said, shaking his head. "If you wait until I've had breakfast, I'll go along and help with the auction."

"I have to tell you, it's not going to be much fun. But since you offer, I accept. Thanks."

"I'm glad I twisted your arm. Now tell me what I've gotten myself into."

Kate explained the cataloging process. "It's not difficult, just nitpicky. We have to be sure all the forms are squared with all the other forms and with the actual merchandise. And there's still a bit of setting up to do. Chairs to unfold, and stuff like that."

"I think I can handle chairs. Is there any particular reason we're doing this?"

"It's another part of the Sesquicentennial celebration. The official ceremonies are tomorrow. My brother is supposed to give a speech, and then there's a reenactment of the founding of the town. Mrs. Bradford is running that."

"Sounds like something I should stick around for," Owen said.

"And there's a beauty pageant tonight. Our maid is one of the contestants and she's a shoo-in as Miss Goober. She always wins."

"Miss . . . Goober?"

"The pageant kicks off the Goober Gala, which starts tomorrow. There will be booths set up around the court square to sell various taste treats made with peanuts."

"Goober Gala . . ." Owen repeated incredulously.

Before Kate could explain the importance of peanuts to the local economy, Carl popped through the door. He hadn't shaved, his eyes were bloodshot, and he'd neglected to change his clothes from the previous evening.

"Hi, guys," he said, and Kate wondered if he had a mouth full of canary.

"What have you been up to?" she asked. "And is it a felony or a misdemeanor?"

"Neither. I didn't get caught." Carl pulled up a chair and straddled it. "Here," he said, offering her a mini tape recorder. "Listen to this."

Kate took it gingerly and pressed the play button, half expecting to hear an obscene phone call he'd bugged. Instead she heard Carl's voice speaking softly and soothingly.

"Hi there," he was saying. "Remember me?"

A girl's voice answered, "No."

"I'm Carl. I was with the policeman who found you on the road."

Kate nearly choked on her coffee. "This is Lynne! How did you manage to get to her?"

"Calm down and listen," Carl growled.

"Oh." Lynne's voice again. "His name is German, you know. Which is kind of weird. I thought maybe his family came from Germany or something. Families do that with names. You see, my full name is Augusta Lynne, because my grandmother was Augusta and my mother's maiden name is Lynne."

She was rambling. No surprise. There was no telling what the girl had been through lately.

"You're mad at him, aren't you?" Lynne went on. "Because he wouldn't let you ride with us."

"It was a long walk," Carl admitted. "But that's not important. I came to find out how you're doing."

"I'm okay," Lynne said doubtfully.

"You know, a lot of people have been looking for you."

"Me, too," Lynne said. "But I got away for a while. I almost made it this time. I felt so clean and so purified. But then the voices came, and I knew it was getting too dangerous."

"Where did the voices come from?"

"They break into my head. Like listening to the radio, but different. I was in my room at that nice inn, when the voice came. From the tree. I thought if I put out the DO NOT DISTURB sign I might get a head start. But there wasn't a sign. Isn't that peculiar?" Lynne sounded breathless, but she went on. "So I had to settle for locking the door."

"And how did you get out of the room?" Carl asked.

"Why, I got out like anyone would. Through the

door. And then I locked it with the nail file from Kate's desk. The voice told me to look for my guardian in the woods."

"And the voice told you to hide from the searchers?"

"They're not really human, you know. They wear masks, but they're not really human. I wonder if they know I'm gone from the inn. They can't go into my private room if it's locked, can they?"

"How can you tell they aren't human?" Carl asked, carefully avoiding her question.

"Oh, that's why I went through the purification. So I could tell. And sometimes I really can, but mostly I get confused because they won't let me be who I really am."

"Who are you, really?" Carl asked.

"I don't know. I *was* Sunshine, but I thought once I found out I'd always know. I thought it would be easy after that and it's not, so maybe I haven't found out yet."

"I see." Carl cleared his throat discreetly. "Would it help any if I told you you're Lynne Hampton?"

"That's what they call me. I know that. But I'm talking about who I *am*."

"Aha." Carl seemed stuck for a reply. "I heard you stayed in a cave for a while. That must have been a pretty scary place."

"We started in the cave, you know. Chained to the walls." Lynne's voice was suddenly firmer, more assured.

"Plato? I guess you're right. Did you see any shadows while you were in the cave? Was anyone in there with you?"

"We're all shadows, existing on flat surfaces. Just images, really, until we make ourselves real."

"Uh-huh. And why were you naked? Any special reason?"

Lynne laughed a little. "Oh, it seemed like a good way to add to the purification. You know, strip away everything that wasn't really me. It was wonderful!"

"So when you take off your clothes, you get real?"

"That's not the first step. First we have to learn everything, and then throw it all away and start fresh."

There was a tapping sound on the tape and a rustle. Then Carl shut the machine off and grinned at Kate.

Owen had listened and now leaned back in his chair, frowning, but silent. Kate, on the other hand, was quite voluble. "Carl Jackson, you scum! How on earth could you do that?"

"Easy," Carl said confidently. "I just picked up a stethoscope from the nurse's desk and wore it around my neck. No one gave me a second look. I walked right in."

"I thought German placed someone outside her door, just to bar people like you."

"Yeah. I made friends with the guard on my way in. But there was a new one when I started to leave, so I wound up spending the night under Lynne's bed."

Kate shook her head. "This tape is illegal. It must be."

"Doesn't matter," Carl insisted. "I did it. I got an exclusive interview with Lynne Hampton."

So he had.

* * *

The school gym was barely a mile to the east of the inn, but before she could begin setting up the auction, Kate had to drive west into town to pick up a few last-minute donations for the sale. "Like they're doing us a great favor," she grumbled. "The video store donated a two-dollar gift certificate. And just look at this." She shoved a shapeless bundle in the space between the front seats. "Eliza Leach donated a bust of Beethoven."

"What's wrong with that?" Owen asked.

"Her son sculpted it when he was in high school. And he was *not* an art major."

"I expect people will bid on anything," Owen said reassuringly. "It's a fund-raiser, after all. Folks buy garbage just to be nice."

"Yeah sure, right. At least we're through collecting. Now the real work starts." Kate glanced into the side mirror and pulled Patrick's van into the center of Primrose Lane. The battered green-and-white pickup that had been weaving its way along the street behind them slowed slightly to let her out. "We'll have to circle the park to get back where we were," she said. "Primrose and Morning Glory are both one-way streets. Another example of intelligent planning. That's the park on the left."

Owen leaned forward to look but saw only a grassy lot with a bench flanked by two young oaks. "That's a park?"

"Best we can do," Kate said, and began the U-turn that would take them around the park and up to the other side on Morning Glory Way. "There's the town statue, by the way. We're saving up for some pigeons to go with it."

Now that they were on the opposite side Owen could see a statue sticking up from the ground. It was small and directly in front of the bench, which explained why he hadn't seen it before. What he still hadn't figured out was, what the hell it *was*.

"What the hell is it?" he asked.

"Water nymph," Kate explained. Both of Owen's eyebrows shot up at that, and she could understand why. The statue appeared to represent an overnourished young woman wrapped in a bedsheet. It stood in the middle of a grassy lawn, and there was no water in sight. "Someone had ordered it from the monument company over in Benton Harbor, then changed his mind. So Jesus Creek got a discount."

"Watch out!" Owen shouted, as the school bus in front of them came to a sudden halt.

"Relax. It's just the senior citizens." Kate came to a full stop behind the bus. The green pickup behind them squealed and lurched, but managed to stop before rear-ending the van. "Once a month someone picks up a bunch of residents from the nursing home, and they get a tour of Jesus Creek. Then they go to lunch, or shopping, or whatever. If you've done any driving in this town, you know to watch out for the bus. They'll probably be at the auction later."

"Not if they don't get their butts in gear. Are they just going to park in the middle of the street?"

"Yep. Ivy's driving the bus and it's easier to leave it right there than to pull over. Did you ever try to steer a busload of old people around one-way streets? Besides, there's plenty of room to pass if you're driving a small car. We just happen to be in a van." Kate turned off the engine and opened her door. "Come on. We'll give them a hand."

By the time Owen had gotten out and carefully locked the passenger door, Kate was already assisting an elderly woman in her descent from the bus. Three more people had to be helped out the door of the bus before Kate and Owen were free to wander around by themselves.

"Would you like to sit on the bench?" Kate asked him. "It might be cooler there."

"I'd like to get in the van and leave," Owen said. "And that fellow in the truck would probably like to do the same."

Kate looked back over her shoulder. The driver of the pickup was revving his engine furiously. "Oh, that's Harvey. He'll figure out eventually that he has to back up and go the long way around. We can't leave until the bus does. Or until Harvey does. Right now he's probably too drunk to care."

Owen grinned. "The town drunk? I thought that was a myth."

"Well, he's not *our* town drunk, you understand. He lives over in Benton Harbor, but he comes into Jesus Creek every few months. The Traditional Faith Church is having a pot luck supper tonight, and he tries not to miss a free meal. Afterward he'll go down to The Drink Tank and tie one on, then he'll go to church in the morning. Sometimes Mrs. Bradford takes him home for lunch. She keeps trying to fix him."

"Fix him?"

"You know. Get him sober. What she doesn't realize is that he needs a good stiff drink to get him through Brother B.'s sermons."

Owen leaned over to read the plaque attached to the base of the Nereid. " 'Bless them in their watery grave'?"

Kate nodded. "You see, once the town got the statue, they had to figure out what to do with it. Finally someone remembered the battle between Confederate forces and the Union navy. It happened just a few miles from here, on the Tennessee River. The Union got massacred, and this statue is supposed to commemorate all those soldiers who drowned."

"Let me get this straight. This is a memorial to the *Union* dead?"

Kate grinned. "Hard to believe, I know. And right after this statue went up, the Sons and Daughters of the Confederacy emptied their treasury to put up a huge Confederate memorial on the courthouse lawn. But they didn't dare complain about this one, because a memorial to the dead Yankees was such a Christian thing to do."

The roar of the pickup's engine caught Owen's attention, and he turned just in time to see the truck jump the curb and tear across the park. It was headed straight for the statue.

"Move!" he shouted, and shoved Kate off her feet, throwing himself on top of her. The pickup flashed past, missing them by less than a foot, and plowed into the water nymph. Harvey didn't stop until he'd landed the truck on top of the park bench.

Kate pushed Owen aside and raised herself on one elbow. "Good God! He could've killed somebody!" She glanced quickly at the gaggle of old people and noted that most of them, half-deaf anyway, didn't seem to have noticed the excitement. They were all bunched around the door of the bus, still trying to get their picnic supplies and folding lawn chairs unpacked. Ivy, the young aide who was herding them around, had certainly noticed, and was making obscene gestures toward the truck.

"Kate! Are you hurt?" Owen was on his hands and knees, frantically inspecting her for injuries.

"I'm fine," she promised. "We'd better check on Harvey, though." Pushing herself up, Kate headed across the park to the pickup. She had to walk carefully around the chunks of water nymph that littered the grass.

Owen had caught up with her by the time she pulled Harvey's door open. "Are you nuts?" he shouted to the man inside. "What the hell did you think you were doing?"

Harvey had his arms wrapped around the steering wheel and his head buried in his arms. His body was trembling, and for a moment Kate thought he might be crying or just plain scared. But when Harvey finally raised his head to look at them, she saw that he was actually laughing. "Goddamn!" he crowed, and laughed again.

"Harvey, can you walk?" Kate asked. "Does anything hurt?"

Harvey shook his head. "I always did hate that statue, didn't you? Knocked the shit out of it, didn't I? Ha!"

"You damn near killed us," Kate pointed out. "Did you have to turn to vandalism at just this moment?"

"What? Oh . . . sorry, lady." Harvey took a deep breath and tried to control his mirth. "I was just trying to get out of here. Some damned fool parked right in front of me, right out there in the middle of the road."

"That was me," Kate explained. "The bus stopped in front of me. Harvey, you can't drive across the park just because someone's holding up traffic."

"I just did."

"Kate, the idiot's too drunk to talk to." Owen pulled her away from the door. "Look, pal. If you're not hurt, then we'll just have the police clean up the mess you've made."

"Hell, no. I'm not hurt. I'll just go on my way. One thing, though. There's a log under my truck. Reckon you can help me get it unstuck?"

"It's a bench," Owen said. "Just stay put and we'll find a winch." Turning to Kate he added, "Patrol cars have winches, don't they?"

"Not that kind," she said. "I think word has spread. That sounds like German now." Sure enough, the whine of a siren seemed to be headed their way. "We'd better keep an eye on Harvey until German gets here."

Kate looked around to see if any other damage had been done. Except for the statue and the bench—and the deep ruts created by Harvey's tires—the park seemed intact. But on Primrose Lane, directly across from the park, Eliza Leach, treasurer of the Sons and Daughters of the Confederacy, stood on her front porch smiling at the debris.

Kate had driven Owen and the last of the donated auction items out to the school gym, fully expecting the rest of the morning to be frantic. They'd wasted a lot of time explaining to German why they were parked in the middle of the street, why Harvey had chosen to run down an unarmed water nymph, and why the nursing home residents were happily eating cheese sandwiches in the middle of the destruction.

With Owen's help the sale items were finally arranged and tagged before noon, and there was, to Kate's amazement, nothing else to do until the auction started.

"I have to stick around until the auctioneer gets here," Kate told him. "But you go find somewhere cool." She dropped into one of the folding chairs and began fanning her face with an index card. "I'll give you the keys to the van, and you can just pick me up later."

"I have nothing special to do, and I don't relish going back into town. Not while those children spout Scripture. Also, I'm developing a phobia about Jesus Creek traffic. And the way people keep disappearing from the inn, I don't want to be alone there. If you don't object, I'll just stick around. This may be the safest place in town."

Don't count on it, Kate thought. She reached across the sale item table for a pewter candlestick and ran her hand absently along the side. "By the way, thanks for the help. And congratulations. You were exactly right about Lynne turning up."

"Thanks, but I didn't do anything."

"Being right counts for a lot. Now you'll have to find the other you."

Owen frowned. "Must I? You wouldn't really make me do *that*."

A brilliant thought had just occurred to her. "Maybe Lynne knows where he is."

Owen picked up a wine glass he'd been studying and ran his index finger gently around the rim. "Why would she know anything?"

"She disappeared, some guy showed up claiming to be you, he disappeared, and then Lynne reappeared. Maybe there's a connection in there somewhere."

"That's another puzzle. Why did this fellow show up here impersonating me? Did he know I'd been released by the Hamptons? Did they hire him? And why my name?"

Kate shrugged. "Maybe it really is his name. . . . Okay, so it's not very likely. Or maybe he was planning to kill you and assume your identity permanently. Or maybe the Hamptons hired you so everyone would know you were coming here, then dumped you and sent in someone they know to impersonate you. So that whatever the psychic found, they could control. Does that makes sense?"

"I understand what you're saying, yes; but no, it doesn't make sense. Don't you think the Hamptons wanted Lynne to be found?"

"I'm not sure. Look, I know Lynne is a little erratic, maybe even certifiable. But from what she said that first night at the inn and from what I heard on the tape, I think she's just trying to figure out who she is. And if that doesn't jibe with what her parents want her to be, who knows? Maybe they'd just as soon have her dead as to let her be who she wants to be."

Owen shook his head. "Would they care that much? Do they?"

"Who knows what massive amounts of money might do to the mind?" Kate said. "Anyway, what about the other Komelecki?"

Owen shrugged. "Beats me."

"Don't you know? Can't you get a feeling about him?"

"You've been watching too many cheap movies. Most of psychic perception is subliminal. Everybody sees the same thing, okay? Some of us just put the pieces together to form a whole picture. And to do that, we have to have the pieces."

"You mean psychics are just like everybody else, only quicker?"

"That's about it. Although I once knew someone who really could predict future events. For example he might know when a plane was going to crash. Once in a while I do have a flash about the future, but it's always iffy."

"So you *can* do it!" Kate said excitedly. "You could work on that ability, strengthen it. . . ."

"Kate, this guy I mentioned finally killed himself. The guilt got him, because he couldn't always predict disaster and even when he did, he often didn't have enough information to prevent it."

"But you would be able to deal with it because it

would be something you'd worked for, not just something thrown at you. And you'd know things."

"I don't want to know."

"It would drive me nuts," Kate said. "Mysteries all over, and you just wander around playing with auction items."

"Mysteries?" Owen put the glass on the table. "It's a mystery why TV networks always cancel your favorite show."

"I'm serious. Don't you wonder? Why are we here? Why do we do what we do? I'll bet if you tried you could find out how big the universe is."

"What good would that do me?"

Kate said impatiently, "The point is, haven't you ever tried to figure this stuff out? Phychically, I mean."

"You don't understand, Kate. I find the concept of a balanced checkbook awesome. I can't handle too much knowledge."

"Okay, then just tell me this: What do you believe in?"

"Serendipity," he said.

Owen whistled under his breath. "Not bad," he said, looking over Kate's shoulder at the tally sheet.

"I think that'll buy a few flower boxes," she said proudly. "The Women's Guild ought to be happy."

They had squeezed into a corner of the gym to watch the auction. Owen had left for a few seconds to bid on the set of wine glasses he'd liked so much. Otherwise he'd shown admirable patience and loyalty.

The auction had gone well so far. It was almost

over, thank goodness, and the bidding was still furious. Even Mrs. Bradford had made a halfhearted
bid on the pink flamingos, but she yielded gracefully to old Mrs. O'Dell.

Clara Maddox, president of the Jesus Creek
Women's Guild, moved in and grabbed Kate's hand.
"Kate, you've done a magnificent job!" she gushed.
"We can't thank you enough for handling this. And
next year I'm sure you'll have all the bugs worked
out."

"Next year? Wait, I'm not—" Kate had begun to
explain that she had no intention of running the
auction again next year, or ever again, when Clara
disappeared back into the crowd.

"Seems they're pleased with your effort," Owen
mused.

"Pleased? *Pleased?* I'm not even a member of
their stupid club—and they think I'm going through
this *again*?"

"If you want to join their club, just tell them."

"I don't want to join. And I don't want to do this
auction again."

"Okay, but don't yell at me. Why did you volunteer in the first place?"

"Well, someone had to do it," Kate said sincerely.

The next item up was a ruffled set of baby doll
pajamas. Estelle Carhart was upping the bid viciously, clearly determined to own those pajamas.
Just what every spinster librarian needs, Kate
thought.

"I think the biddies are tickled with you, kid."
Eloise wandered up to pat Kate's arm.

"Clara Maddox thinks I'm doing this again next year. Boy, is she in for a rude awakening."

"They'll convince you. Mark what I'm telling you. Clara's husband's the best lawyer in the county, and she's learned all about persuasion from him."

"Listen, Eloïse, I need to ask you about this date Glenda had with Komelecki."

"I never said they had a date. They just came in together and sat at the same table. In fact Glenda didn't look too happy about the situation. I've got to pick up my satin sheets. Got 'em for practically nothing." Eloise disappeared before Kate could determine whether she meant the price or the use.

"So your maid met up with the guy? That's interesting. She hasn't gone missing, has she?"

"I saw her at work this morning. Can you believe that? I told her she could take the day off to get ready for the pageant, but she insisted on working."

The atmosphere in the room had suddenly turned hostile, Kate realized, and she looked up to see what had happened. Brother B. was bidding against Charlie Moody for a set of radial tires. Or Brother B. *had been* bidding. Apparently Charlie had not seen fit to give in graciously to clergy, and Mrs. Bradford, angry and offended, had entered the fray. She was bidding quickly and heatedly, upping Charlie's every bid with one of her own while her husband sat by, calmly waiting for the outcome.

"I do want to ask Glenda about Komelecki," Kate said to Owen. "But she's got the pageant, and I hate to bother her."

Charlie had finished up the bidding, and now he

was winding his way through the crowded room to tag the tires. Kate glanced quickly at Mrs. Bradford to see how she'd taken the loss. Not well.

Verna Prince was the next to find Kate and Owen huddled in the corner. "Kate, how are you? I've heard you've got a psychic at your place."

"Well, yes," Kate said. "In fact, this—"

"Looking for the Hampton girl. Uh-huh, well, I wonder if he'll have any luck. Sad, isn't it?"

"Lynne's been found, you know. She—"

"Really? Well, isn't that wonderful? Uh-huh, and I guess she's all right then."

"Yes, she's in—"

"The hospital. I guess so. Such a tragedy, don'tcha think? Poor girl. Poor little rich girl." Verna's attention had wandered to the conversation behind her, and before Kate could try again she'd turned her head away.

"What was that?" Owen asked.

"Hurricane Verna. Notice how peaceful it is now that she's gone?"

"In Jesus Creek, a hurricane could be considered a quiet day," Owen said. "You people sure lead exciting lives."

Kate wondered what on earth the man meant. Oh, sure. A few people disappeared, a mob of reporters held court on somebody's lawn, drunken lunatics assaulted innocent old people, and . . . well, come to think of it, she could see his point.

Sunday had begun with great promise. J.C. had installed the new air-conditioning unit the day before, and the inn was blissfully cool. And quiet. The students of the Christian School had finally finished their struggle with Revelation. That in itself was enough to inspire Kate to get out and attend the noon speech her brother was scheduled to give.

She was somewhat surprised to learn that he had indeed arrived. Having come directly from the airport to the court square, he jabbered on and on (as good politicians do) about the fine community that had been built along the banks of Jesus Creek, about the wonderful people who currently inhabited the community, and about the numerous (albeit unnamed) accomplishments of his term. Kate applauded his arrival, if not his speech.

Most of the citizens had turned out, despite the heat, either to hear Patrick or, more probably, to watch the reenactment of the founding of Jesus Creek. Lindsay James Leach, the editor of the weekly *Jesus Creek Headlight*, was covering the event and apparently loving every minute of it. He'd worked for the paper for years, when his father had been the owner. Now Lindsay James was fresh out of college and running the show. He waved at Kate, then turned back to his notebook.

Most of the townsfolk had dressed themselves in pioneer costumes. Kate assumed this was some sort of misguided tribute to the Founding Fathers. Kate herself was wearing more sensible clothing, and she figured the early pioneers would have, too, if they'd had the option.

She had no trouble spotting Owen in the crowd. He was the one with cutoff jeans and a sunburned head.

"Taking pictures, I see," she said, moving in behind him. "Planning to preserve the event for our own descendants, so they can reenact the reenactment?"

"Hi. Missed you at breakfast." He was fiddling with his camera and didn't look up.

"I'm not into morning, remember? You should've set up a photography booth. Photos for a buck, or something. I'll bet these people would love to have their picture taken in costume—or maybe the dirty old men would like theirs taken with Miss Goober."

"Did Glenda win?"

"Didn't you see her? She was on stage with Patrick. The sun glinting off her crown nearly blinded me."

"Oh." Owen cleared his throat. "Sorry. I was late getting started. Afraid I missed your brother's remarks."

"Don't apologize. With any forethought I'd have been late, too."

"Smile," he said, and snapped her picture.

"Good grief. You're one of those sneaky ones. Don't do that."

"Sorry, but you looked like a poser. I'd rather capture the true you."

"Come on." Kate took his arm. "Put that thing away and let's grab a good spot along the creek bank." She pulled him across the courtyard and marched him down the sidewalk on Morning Glory Way. The one-way street had been closed to traffic for the day, to allow room for the reenactment.

"How long does this take?" Owen asked, tugging at the collar of his shirt.

"How should I know? I've never been to a Sesquicentennial before. The original production involved forty or so religious pilgrims. I assume the reenactment will be fairly accurate. But whether they'll be baptized together or separately, I don't know."

"Baptized? Isn't that rather a strange way to celebrate a birthday?"

"Oh," Kate said, realizing that he had no idea what to expect. "You see, the first settlers were led by Hiram Wicken. See, here we are on Wicken Street; guess who it's named for? Notice also that it's a dead end. Sort of like Wicken's commune. Anyway, they came from New England in the early part of the nineteenth century, hoping to find religious toleration if not freedom. I think they'd already figured out that they weren't going to find that."

"Wait a minute," Owen said. "They had a commune?"

"Oh, sure. That's why they were run out of wherever they were in the first place. So they came here, and Wicken decided this was the ideal place. They stopped to pray, one assumes, then slogged into the water and baptized each other."

"And your Mrs. Bradford approves of this commune thing?"

"Not a *commune* commune. This was a *religious* commune. Very straitlaced. Right down Mrs. Bradford's alley, in fact. Literally. She lives at the end of Wicken Street."

"I gather they've already baptized and drowned those miserable brats who were reading aloud. And good riddance." Owen swatted at a fly that was buzzing around his neck.

"Mercy. This heat has made you nasty."

"This isn't heat," Owen argued. "This is hell."

"Sure is," agreed a man dressed in buckskin.

They watched as the members of the Jesus Creek Traditional Faith Church began their procession along Wicken Street and down to the creek, singing "Onward, Christian Soldiers."

"Hard tune to carry," Kate said in response to Owen's grimace. She noted that Miss Constance Winter was bringing up the rear, but since the woman was not in costume Kate assumed she was not an official part of the reenactment. The best part of being crazy, Kate thought, is that Miss Constance and others like her are able to join in anywhere they feel compelled. And the best part about being crazy in Jesus Creek was that no one would question Miss Constance's participation.

Brother B., of course, had been cast in the role of Hiram Wicken. He gathered the others around him and spent the next ten minutes fulsomely relating the story of how a handful of the faithful had left their home in New England in search of religious freedom in the South. Then, with a theatrical wave, Brother B. announced, "This is the home our Father hath chosen for us. We dedicate this ground and our hearts to the Lord."

The crowd on shore applauded listlessly. Kate noticed Glenda in a strapless sun dress and crown, standing on a stump. Her applause was especially bubbly, but then Glenda knew how to give a crowd what it wanted, and she always took her responsibilities seriously.

All the actors, at a nod from Mrs. Bradford, gave a solemn amen and bowed their heads. Brother B. stretched out a hand to his wife, and together they walked into the rapidly roiling creek. The water was probably a great relief to both of them, Kate decided, dressed as they were. In fact the rest of the crowd looked ready to jump in, too.

Standing knee-deep in the water, Brother B. reached up to place his hand on Mrs. Bradford's head. Kate wondered if she'd remember to tuck that long skirt between her knees before it caught an air bubble. Brother B. shouted out something about the sincerity with which they gave themselves to the fulfillment of their commitment to God. All the while he was struggling to remain standing in the rushing water.

Kate was impressed. The reenactment had been completely written and produced by Mrs. Bradford. Her husband proved to be an excellent actor, with none of the uncertain inflection common to amateurs.

"O Lord," Brother B. was saying, "we begin our new life, cleansed by the Holy Spirit." He was thoroughly caught up in his role, and paid no attention to the rumbles and whispers that started at one end of the crowd and moved along like a wave. "Father, wash away our sins!" he shouted, and dipped his wife backward into the water.

Everyone on shore saw the clump of brush and dark fabric break loose from the roots of a tree that had grown out over the creek. Isn't it funny, Kate thought as the water carried it gracefully along, that no one is saying anything?

And because they weren't, Mrs. Bradford went unwarned. She leaned back into the water and found herself baptized in the pale, bloated, and very dead arms of Owen Komelecki the First.

Realizing immediately that something wasn't right, Mrs. Bradford tried to stand up. Thrashing and coughing, she fought the pull of the body that had gotten tangled in her billowing pioneer skirts. Brother B. worked valiantly to free his wife from the grotesque snare while she clung fiercely to him, screaming and gurgling and spitting water.

Kate realized that the crowd had grown still. She saw Glenda, pale as a statue under her carefully acquired tan. The bona fide Owen had been prepared to take a picture of the baptism, but his finger had frozen on the camera. Eloise stood with her hand at her throat, a sudden breeze blowing her curls away from her shoulders. Everyone seemed frozen in place except for Roger Shelton, who had grabbed Delia Cannon by the shoulders and was attempting to turn her away from the horrible sight.

Finally someone said, "Oh, God."

CHAPTER

6

NO ONE FELT MUCH LIKE GOING FOR A swim after all. Most of the crowd seemed oblivious to the heat as they huddled together, watching the body being dragged from the water and then wrapped in a plastic sheet. German and his deputy had attempted to rope off the area where the body had washed up, but the unruly throng kept trampling over the nylon cord to take snapshots and gawk.

Kate watched the body being loaded into an ambulance and noted with satisfaction that she didn't feel faint or queasy, or any of the anguish she'd felt when she saw Anne's body. Her reaction to that had been embarrassing. One quick glance at the bullet hole in Anne's head and Kate had started screaming like a banshee. For ten or fifteen minutes the other members of Patrick's victory party had tried to calm her. Eventually they'd succeeded in getting her quiet, but then Kate had thrown up all over Patrick.

The body in the creek had looked much worse than Anne's, but Kate barely noticed the flutter in her stomach. Obviously she was learning to cope with stress, and she attributed this improvement to the many books and educational pamphlets she'd been reading.

German approached her wearing his serious-business expression. "I hate to ask," he said, "you being a girl and all. But we need somebody to come down to the morgue and ID this guy."

"The morgue? I didn't even know we had one."

German's face was flushed from the heat and he looked apologetic. "Well, actually we take 'em to the ER, and the doctor on call pronounces 'em dead. But I still need somebody to ID the deceased."

"German, I can't identify him," Kate argued. "I didn't even know who he was when he was alive."

"I'll identify him," Owen said quietly.

German and Kate both turned to stare at him, and Kate said, "But you never even met Komelecki."

"That is not another Owen Komelecki," Owen promised. "His name is Robert Sanderson. Until about two weeks ago he was my assistant. It was just after the Hamptons supposedly called, come to think of it, that he quit."

"Ohhh," Kate said. "So *that's* it. You think?"

"He lied about their contacting me. And I don't imagine he called them back, either." Owen smiled wryly.

"What the hell are you two talking about?" German demanded.

Owen turned to German and explained. "The assistant who was working for me—Sanderson, that is—claimed to have received a phone call from the Hamptons. He said they'd canceled the assignment. Obviously he made that up, intending to take my place here. Don't ask me why."

"Really?" German squinted at Owen, which indicated that he was probably thinking. "You and this Sanderson have a falling-out before you fired him?"

"I didn't fire him. He quit. And no, we didn't have any disagreements. I never liked him much, but he was a capable assistant. Efficient, great with clients."

"Well, we'll have to see about that, won't we?" German hooked his thumbs into his gun belt, spit a stream of tobacco juice across the street, and squinted again. Kate supposed he was trying to intimidate Owen.

Owen wasn't easily intimidated. "The question is, how did he wind up dead?"

"I guess that's what we'll be trying to find out." German started for his patrol car, then remembered that he needed someone to identify the body. "Both of you, come with me," he said.

Owen and Kate hopped into the backseat, hoping to enjoy a cool ride to the hospital. It figured that German's car didn't have an air conditioner, and the back windows, of course, couldn't be rolled down.

"I don't know about you," Kate said, fanning herself with her hand, "but I'm just about tired of this game."

"Yeah," Owen agreed. "If things don't start getting better real soon, I'm taking my marbles home."

After Kate and Owen had identified the body, German dragged them back to his office. Now they were all jammed in, jockeying for the spot nearest the air conditioner. German propped his feet up on his desk, inadvertently knocking the Styrofoam spit cup over onto a stack of papers. He didn't seem to notice.

"Have you talked to Glenda?" Kate asked. "Eloise said she was in the diner with Komelecki—excuse me, Sanderson—the night he disappeared."

"Now, Katie," German said, "you don't think a purty thing like Glenda could have anything to do with this?"

"If Glenda *had* killed him, she'd have gotten away with it." Lest the deputy take her statement seriously, Kate continued: "No, German, I don't think a purty thing like Glenda is responsible. But it's possible that she knows where he was going after they parted company."

"Reckon he went to the river. What's the mystery in that?"

"And what do you think happened then?" Owen asked.

"Well"—German leaned back in his chair—"we figure the Hampton girl killed him. You know that cave where we found her clothes? Right on the creek there. Seems to me this-here Sanderson was walking along the path. You remember the secret path, Kate? He probably spotted the girl there and went after her, and then she whacked him over the head.

If it was self-defense there won't be much of a case against her."

"My God! If she'd had a sledgehammer, she couldn't have done *that* to him. And by the way," Kate said, "did you find any deadly weapons in the cave?"

German shook his head impatiently. "Not a thing. But whatever she bashed him with, it's probably down in the creek somewhere. A big rock, maybe. We'll get out there and drag for it, I guess."

Kate wasn't happy with German's conclusions. She didn't think Sanderson was the sort to attack women physically, although that was difficult to predict sometimes. And Lynne surely would have mentioned the experience during her babbling, but Kate couldn't tell German about that without getting Carl into trouble. "I think you need to investigate other possibilities before you accuse Lynne Hampton of murder. After all, her family could make your life a living hell if they wanted."

"Tell you what," German drawled, "if you come up with any evidence to point to someone else, you let me know. In the meantime I'll decide who's guilty."

Kate and Owen left on foot, after deciding that there was no point in trying to reason with German. He'd offered them a ride, but even the scorching afternoon sun was preferable to spending another minute with German Hunt.

"He's wrong, isn't he?" Kate asked Owen.

"Probably."

"Do you know who did it?"

"Possibly."

"Then tell me."

Owen shook his head. "Not yet, Kate. I hate to be vague, and I'm not deliberately keeping you in the dark, but I'm afraid this situation will grow even worse before it's over. And besides, I haven't figured out what the motive could be. I may be off on this one. It happens sometimes, especially if I let myself get involved."

"How are you involved? You had nothing to do with it."

"I mean involved with the other people around here. I usually go in, find what I'm looking for, and ride into the sunset. But here I am walking around with you, setting up auctions with you. Let's say . . . you're the killer. I'd have to decide whether to turn you in or cover for you. Either way, I lose."

Kate stopped just before reaching the steps of the inn. The lawn was empty, all the reporters having moved down the road to the area where Sanderson's body had been discovered. "But you know I didn't do it. So why is there a problem?"

"I've met several people here already. Some I like, some I don't, but the point is, I'm not objective anymore. I have to figure out whether I'm reading the situation accurately or not." He opened the front door and let Kate step inside.

Patrick was draped comfortably across a chair, freshly showered, dressed in his wealthy-man-at-home attire, and sipping iced tea. Kate noticed that his tan was still in place, so he'd evidently found a tanning salon during his trip. Patrick didn't like to let his color slip.

"It's about time you showed up," she told him. "Where are you when all these disasters start?"

"Hello, Katherine. Good to see you, too." Patrick saluted Owen with his tea glass.

"Hello, Patrick. Nice campaign speech. Now, hang out your Innkeeper-in-Residence sign. I refuse to be responsible for this place anymore." Kate wished she had something appropriate to throw to underscore her words.

"You're right, Katherine. We've got to do something here. People disappear, guests wind up dead. It's not good for business."

Kate turned to Owen. "It's not good for business," she repeated.

"Are you the psychic?" Patrick stood to shake Owen's hand. "Good to meet you," he said, suddenly enthusiastic. "Listen, I don't suppose you could give me a handle on this. We need to find out who's responsible for this murder, straighten matters out, before the inn is ruined."

"The police think Lynne Hampton killed him," Owen said cautiously. "I don't know what evidence they have but—"

"Now, that might work. Lynne and this Sanderson had arranged to meet here; they had some sort of lovers' quarrel and she killed him. I certainly can't be held responsible for that."

"Damn it, Patrick, stop! Forget about your precious public image and what looks good! You're always trying to avoid responsibility for things!" Kate paused, having run out of breath.

"Calm down, Katherine. Every time I talk to you lately you seem on the verge of hysteria. Maybe it's the heat." Patrick returned to his chair and propped his feet on a table.

"It is *not* the heat," she said through clenched teeth. "It's you."

"Excuse me," Owen said quietly, somewhat daunted by the family feud. "I think I'll run upstairs and take a nap."

"We certainly hope you enjoy your stay!" Patrick called cheerily after him.

Within the hour German and J.D., the only other cop on daytime duty, showed up to search Sanderson's room. Owen and Kate stood in the doorway, watching as the two rummaged recklessly through closet, desk drawers, and suitcases.

"Looky here," German said, and whistled. He'd found the stack of newspaper clippings and magazines that Kate was already familiar with. But German's search was more thorough than the one Carl and Owen had conducted. He found another pile of clippings stashed away in Sanderson's suitcase and handed one to Kate.

"This is just another article about Lynne," she said, passing the note to Owen.

"Uh-huh, but the rest of these are all about the Hampton family. Looks like this guy dug up a lot of dirt."

Kate stepped forward to look over German's shoulder and saw that he was right. He had a handful of newspaper and magazine articles about the family.

Across the room J.D. dumped a drawerful of paper on the floor. A pile of what had been neatly arranged file folders slid across the colonial blue carpet. Kate could see that one was full of items about Owen, and one folder was marked PATRICK MCCULLOUGH. Just beside it was a sheet of paper labeled KATE YANCY. She picked it up and scanned the notes Sanderson had made. He'd somehow obtained the dates of her marriage and divorce, her ex-husband's current address, and figures from her last income tax return.

"Did you check this weirdo out at all before you hired him?" she asked.

Owen shook his head. "For what I pay I can't afford to be choosy."

"Well, I've got news for you. You should *get* choosy. This guy was a real nut."

German looked up and laughed. "You mean you just now noticed? I caught on to it right away, when he barged into my office and said he wanted to mind-meld with the computer."

"Doesn't matter," Kate said. "Whatever his intentions, his dirty work is over now. But I don't like the idea of some stranger having access to my private life." She held up the folder that contained her tax return.

"Why should it bother you, Katie?" German asked. "You've lived a squeaky-clean life. Still, nut or no, somebody killed the man. I mean to find out who."

"When will Reb be back?" Kate asked. "Maybe you should call him and tell him to cut his vacation short."

"Reb's off in the wilderness somewhere. No way to get hold of him when he takes off like that. Be-

sides, I can handle this." German seemed miffed at
her lack of confidence in him.

"If you'd like," Owen offered, "I'll call my assistant and have her send Sanderson's résumé to you.
I don't know that any of the information will be
accurate, but it might be worth a look."

German's eyes narrowed. "You're mighty help-
ful, aren't you? You got something you're trying to
steer me away from?"

"I'm the good guy. If you don't want my help . . ."

"Okay," German said, still eyeing Owen. "Send
me that résumé. Meanwhile, you plan on staying
here in town until this is cleared up."

Kate dragged Owen back downstairs for a conference while German and J.D. finished packing up
Sanderson's possessions. "Look," she said as they
reached the entry hall, "German isn't too bright. If
you don't give him a lead, and I'm talking a brick
on the head, he's just stupid enough to arrest you.
Or me."

"You he won't bother. He's decided you're above
suspicion. For all you know *I* may be a serial
killer."

"That's ridiculous. Why would you murder Sanderson?"

"For starters, he soiled my good name."

Kate raised an eyebrow. "Soiled?"

"Yes, soiled. And he had a file on me. Could have
been blackmail. He worked for me. Maybe he set
me off with his touch typing."

"Very funny, Owen. Can you at least tell me who
or what you suspect?"

"How do I know I can trust you? As I've said, I can't even trust my own senses now."

Kate sighed.

"How far is this place?" Carl asked, slipping on a loose rock.

"Just down here." Kate pointed into a dark section of trees. "It only seems long because of the overgrown path. When I was a kid we all used this for a secret hideout, and the path was worn clear."

"What happened? People in this town stop having kids?"

"The video arcade on Main Street is more popular than trailblazing." Kate stopped and pretended to consider the best way to proceed. She didn't want Carl to know that she was out of breath already.

"Then how did the Hampton girl find the cave?"

"Probably just followed the creek. If she walked along the bank, she couldn't have missed it."

Carl glared at her. "Then why aren't we walking along the bank?"

Kate gave him a contemptuous look. "Because anybody can find it that way. We're taking the secret path."

"Well it's not very secret, is it, if the Hampton girl just found it by accident?"

"The *cave's* not secret. The path is." Kate started walking again, a little slower this time. "We used to cover it with limbs and leaves, but I imagine everyone knew about it anyway. There it is."

"Where?" Carl squinted against the sunlight filtering in through the trees.

"Around there. Take off your shoes. We'll have

to go into the water and climb up." Kate slipped off her own shoes and waded in.

"You didn't tell me this was an endurance test." Carl followed her, grumbling about the cold water, the slippery rocks, and the fish that nibbled his toes.

It had been a long time since Kate had climbed up the rocky bank to the cave. She found that the niches had gotten smaller and harder to grasp, and her arms no longer had the strength to pull her body effortlessly into the opening. Carl grew tired of waiting and gave her bottom a firm shove, sending her sprawling into the mouth of the cave.

Once inside, she turned to face him and was gratified to see that he fell in face-forward. "I could have made it by myself."

"Oh, sure," Carl said, rolling over onto his back. "I've done it a million times."

"Yeah, but how often since you became an old maid?"

"Look, Mr. Bernstein-Woodward, I'm doing you a favor. I've got better things to do with my time. There's an accountant who's expecting me to—"

"All right. Thanks for doing me this huge favor." Carl stood up and dusted off his pants. "Now look around, and let's see if she left anything behind."

"The cops have already picked the place clean," Kate protested.

"You never know," Carl said absently. "How far back does this go?"

"Not very. You don't think our mothers would have let us hang around a real cave? This is just a little dent in the hill."

Carl bumped his head on the low rock ceiling. He swore, then bent forward in an awkward position.

"See?" Kate said smugly. "I was smart enough to stay on my knees."

"Good for you. Think you could move over a little? You're blocking the light."

Kate sat down against the damp wall and hugged her knees to her chest, while Carl gave the cave a careful search. He crawled along the floor, running his fingers up and down the slimy sides. She hoped he met up with a hostile reptile.

Somewhere in all of this, Kate thought, there is reason. Some explanation. Why did Sanderson call himself Komelecki? If he had wanted to play psychic, he could have used his own name. As it was, he'd only publicized the real Komelecki.

Kate wrinkled her nose. Now, there was an unpleasant thought. Maybe this mess had started as a publicity stunt. But then, why was Sanderson killed? And those files in his room were another mystery. Why had he researched the citizens of Jesus Creek so meticulously—blackmail? In Patrick's case maybe that was feasible. Her brother would accede to any demand, so long as his precious image remained untarnished. But despite what the media would have her believe, Kate didn't think anyone else in town cared much about protecting their secrets. When you came right down to it, there probably weren't any *real* secrets in all of Jesus Creek.

None of it seemed any clearer, she realized, and the strenuous contemplation had made her head hurt. As far as she knew Sanderson hadn't had time to blackmail anyone. Of course, if he'd had an accomplice . . .

Hmmm, she said to herself. An accomplice. And suppose he'd gone to meet that accomplice the night he died. But who in Jesus Creek would have been in cahoots with Sanderson?

"Damn!" Carl said at last.

"Any luck?"

"There's nothing here but mud and bugs. Hard to believe the heiress lived in this place for . . . what? Three weeks?"

"Yeah. What did she eat, I wonder? I guess she could drink creek water, but what about food? Or maybe she didn't eat. Maybe giving up food is part of her spiritual progress."

"Look." Carl sat down at the mouth of the cave and pointed off to the left.

Kate scooted over beside him. "That's Wicken Street. So?" From where they sat Kate could look down the creek and see the string of shabby houses built along the bank.

"Backyards. I'll bet nobody in this town ever locks a back door."

"Why should we?" Kate asked defensively.

"The point is, Lynne Hampton could easily have crossed the creek and sneaked into any of those houses for food."

"Oh. I see what you mean. Poor girl!"

"Huh?"

"That house there—the one at the end, the one practically falling into the creek. That's the Bradford's place. If Lynne got hold of Mrs. Bradford's leftovers, it's a wonder she was able to survive at all."

As if on cue, Brother B. and his wife emerged from their back door and drifted into the few feet of ground that passed for a yard. Brother B. was wearing Bermuda shorts, something Kate could hardly believe even now as she was seeing it. He and Mrs. Bradford walked around the vegetable patch that covered most of the yard, apparently checking its progress. Mrs. Bradford, still in the handmade print dress she'd worn to work that morning, stooped to pull a few weeds from the tomato row. Brother B. watched and pointed out a few she'd missed. Mrs. Bradford dutifully extirpated the holdout weeds with a quick twist.

Kate stood up and waved her arms above her head. "Hello, Brother B.!" she shouted.

The Bradfords stopped and looked up, trying to find her.

"Over here!" Kate shouted again. "The cave!"

Brother B. raised his arm and returned her wave, but Mrs. Bradford turned back to her garden. Brother B. wandered closer to the house, where he could stand in the minimal shade provided by the back porch.

"Now how am I supposed to get a shot of this?" Carl was studying the layout of the cave.

"You'll have to cross the creek and stand on the other bank."

"Cross the creek? You couldn't have brought me up the other side to start with?"

"Well, how was I supposed to know you wanted pictures?"

"You thought I was just carrying this camera for fun?"

"Look, I brought you to the cave. That's all I can do. Now sit here or take a swim or whatever you want, but I'm going back home. I've got work to do." Kate slid easily down the smooth rock side and into the water, leaving Carl to negotiate the creek by himself.

"At least this one gave me warning before she quit," Owen said as he eased the car into the flow of interstate traffic. "Usually my assistants just don't show up for work one day—and there I am."

When Kate had returned to the inn, still carrying her shoes and wearing jeans that were soaked from the knees down, she'd found Owen waiting for her. When he'd invited her to ride along to his office in Jackson, she couldn't resist. She wondered what a psychic's office would look like, and besides, what else did she have to do? Just receipts and final cleanup after the auction, and maybe interviewing potential maids to carry some of Glenda's work load.

"I'm beginning to think you have a serious character flaw," she said. "How many assistants do you go through in a year, anyway?"

"Oh, four or five. What's that got to do with my character?"

"Well, people don't normally scare off so much hired help in so short a time. Are you bad-tempered or something? Do you throw furniture?"

"Knives." Owen steered left to allow another car onto the highway. "Actually I'm a pussycat. I just have an erratic schedule. Like now—I've left Toni in charge and, frankly, she isn't the type to handle responsibility. She's bright, just refuses to make her own decisions."

"Then why did you hire her in the first place?" Kate asked.

"She answered the ad first."

"That's it?"

"And she has great buns. I always look for that in an employee."

Kate eyed him thoughtfully. "Is that why you hired Sanderson? Maybe I don't know you at all."

"Keeps you on your toes, doesn't it?" Owen turned and grinned at her.

"What worries me is, you sound like Patrick. He has an erratic schedule, so he leaves me to handle everything. And dealing with responsibility isn't my best quality either."

"How long have you been working for him?" Owen asked.

"About two years. I started before the inn opened. Patrick was constantly on the move then, too. Of course, he was campaigning for mayor at the time. At first Anne was doing the renovation. That's Patrick's wife. But when she died, I inherited the job. I decorated all the rooms that aren't proper period. I don't know a Windsor from a wench."

"Two years. So you've been handling responsibilities for two years without ruining the business?"

"Well, yes," Kate admitted, "unless you count disappearing guests and dead bodies."

"And what did you do before?"

"Before I ran the inn?" Kate stalled, trying to

organize an answer that was accurate, if not completely truthful. "I was sort of married."

Owen gave her a puzzled glance. "Sort of?"

"I was. He wasn't." Kate knew she was squirming. One of the human potential books she'd read explained that uncomfortable reactions to past situations may be rooted in the reluctance to let go of said situations. "The plain facts sound so petty. I mean, he didn't beat me or drink up the money or anything. All in all he was a pretty nice guy."

"Forgive me," Owen said gently, "and please don't think I'm being judgmental, but why would you dump a nice guy?"

"I hate this phrase, but I guess we grew apart. We started out with this grand and glorious concept of marriage: my body would be his body; my thoughts would be his thoughts."

"I suppose it got crowded."

Kate shook her head. "Just the opposite. One day I woke up and there I was, all alone. And differences! I wanted a baby; he wanted a Harley. I wanted to grow veggies; he wanted to grow cannabis."

"But they say opposites attract."

"They do. They just can't live together. I mean, sooner or later, you have to find some common ground. Unfortunately, it never occurred to me that just because I was in love I didn't necessarily have to marry the guy."

Owen nodded. "And so you're hanging around the inn waiting for what?"

"I'm not waiting for anything. I'm getting myself in shape emotionally to deal with the world. I'm not going to make the same mistakes over and over again."

"You can't fool me," Owen said, shaking a finger at her. "I'm a psychic."

"Ha! You can't even read minds."

"In your case I don't have to. You have the loudest eyes."

Kate leaned over and looked at herself in the rearview mirror.

"Every time you tell a lie you bat your lashes a few extra times," Owen explained.

"I never lie," Kate said, lowering her head.

"Of course you do, but mostly to yourself. Trust me. I make a living from this. Most of the impressions I get come from my observations of human behavior and body language."

"That doesn't sound very mystical to me."

Owen sighed heavily. "You don't respect me now."

"Of course I respect you. Why shouldn't I?"

"Kate, my girl, I'm a fat bald guy with a ten-year-old car and a laughable bank account. The only ace I've got is this strange ability to find dead bodies and lost dogs."

Kate would have disagreed, except that he *was* bald and he *was* tubby, and if he'd had any money surely he'd have bought a car without rust holes. She patted his arm soothingly. "Your secret's safe with me. That is, if you tell me who murdered Sanderson."

"Really, Kate, I'd expected better of you."

"Don't try to make me feel guilty, Owen. It won't work. I've read *Shedding Guilt*."

"Is that another of your psychobabble books?"

"It happens to be very instructive. How do you expect to grow if you don't read the experts?"

"How do you grow if you only read and don't do it?"

"I *do* do it," Kate insisted. "I mean not just now. But I will. First I want to get everything figured out."

"And what will you do when you do do it?"

"That's one of the things I'm working on. As soon as I decide what I want from life I'll be ready to go after it. I'll be ready to actualize it instead of just accepting the concept on a superficial level. There are nine steps to figuring out what you want. Would you like me to go over them?"

"No, please," Owen begged. "I may have already screwed up, and I'd rather not know."

"Oh, it's not too late!" she said excitedly. "There's a book called *Changing Courses in Mid-Stream. . . .*"

"Please don't be offended, Kate, but I don't want to read any of your books. Just let me muddle along my unenlightened path."

"But, Owen, you could be happy."

"I am happy."

"No you're not." Kate would have expected him to recognize that, but people were so blind to their own problems. "Nobody's ever really happy. We all have areas in our lives that are less than satisfactory."

"Okay, but don't point mine out to me. There's a good chance I'll never notice."

Really, Kate thought with frustration, some people are so pigheaded.

Owen's office was on the third floor of an old brick building. Having plodded up the narrow stairs, they came to a narrower hallway with wooden floors that creaked and sagged beneath their feet. The office itself was barely larger than a closet. Two desks were jammed in side by side, and one entire corner held a collection of cameras, tripods, and lights.

The tall blonde behind the desk had to be Toni-of-the-buns, Kate figured. She was leaning over, trying to open a drawer that was stubbornly resisting her efforts. "Oh, hi, Mr. K." Her voice was as wispy as the strand of hair that fell across her eyes. "I'm really sorry about quitting like this, but the shirt factory called and once I start making production there, the money will double what I—Well, I couldn't turn down the offer."

"Don't worry about it, Toni," Owen said. "You've already been a great help."

"I can stay till the end of the week," she offered.

"Great. Could you do me a favor? If I'm not back by closing time Friday, just put up the GONE FISHING sign."

"Sure thing. Is there anything else?"

"Have you got that check from the Hamptons yet? Good. Stick it in an envelope and mail it back."

"What?" Toni and Kate exclaimed together.

Owen looked from one to the other with obvious surprise. "Well, you don't expect me to keep it. I didn't do anything."

"But Mr. K, the light bill is due next week, you know. And don't forget the invoice on that—"

"Just send it back, Toni. Thanks." Owen squeezed in behind the desk and started rumaging through the battered file cabinet. "Aha!" he said triumphantly. "Toni, you've performed a miracle. Here's Sanderson's application, in the file marked *job applications*?"

"Where else would it be?" Kate asked.

"Before Toni organized the files, it could have been anywhere. I once found a check behind the radiator." He patted Toni's shoulder. "And good luck at the shirt factory."

"Thanks, Mr. K. It's been really nice working for you."

After wiggling his way back to the front of the desk, Owen took Kate's arm and led her to the hallway. He turned back and said to Toni, "If you ever need a job, you've got my number," then pulled the door closed.

"She's charming," Kate said. "And she respects you."

"Big deal. She's leaving me." Owen held up the application form and ran his finger down the list of Robert Sanderson's previous employers. "Okay, says here his last employer was Black and Black Wholesale Meats in Benton Harbor."

"Do you think he told the truth about that?" Kate asked.

"Who'd make up a story about working in a slaughterhouse?"

"Oh, I don't know. Maybe someone who'd claim to be Owen Komelecki."

"You're very suspicious. Probably lack of food. We'll grab a bite and then stop off in Benton Harbor on the way back to Jesus Creek."

Kate paused at the top of the stairway. "What? I thought you were giving that application to German."

"I am. But we might as well save him some time. We're going through Benton Harbor anyway." He started down the stairs, but Kate grabbed his shoulder to stop him.

"Let me get this straight," she said. "You already know who killed Sanderson, but you're still going to do German's job for him?"

"I'm not positive," Owen reminded her. "Maybe if I get more information, construct a kind of motive."

"What has a slaughterhouse got to do with motive?"

"I don't know. But it's a strange job for a man like Sanderson. He didn't seem cut out for manual labor. Can you think of a motive for someone to kill him? Because if you can, I'd love to hear it."

"Maybe someone thought he was you," Kate said. "I'm serious. He claimed to be you. I, for one, certainly never doubted it. Any number of people might have a reason to get nervous about a psychic. You know, believing he could reveal deep dark secrets? The murderer wouldn't even have to be someone from Jesus Creek, just someone who knew you were going to be there."

"But what secrets could he have revealed? There's the sticker. I can't imagine . . . Hell, let's eat. Are you in the mood for tacos or burgers?"

* * *

Judging by outward appearances, Black and Black Wholesale Meats would make ideal grist for a crusading journalist's hot dog exposé. There was a tiny front room carved out of the immense warehouse, and Kate and Owen huddled together in the middle of it, trying not to brush up against the grimy counter.

"If this is any indication of what the back looks like," Kate whispered as she tried to scrape a piece of gum off her shoe, "then these people are single-handedly responsible for most of the food poisoning cases in this state."

Owen gingerly tapped the bell that read RING FOR SERVICE and stepped back, rubbing his hand on his shirt. "Don't they have health inspectors for these places?"

Before Kate could reply, the door marked EMPLOYEES ONLY opened and someone, presumably one of the Blacks, hobbled out. He was painfully thin, a clear indication to Kate that running a slaughterhouse had ruined his appetite. He was also older than any human had a right to be.

"May I help you?" he croaked.

"Are you Mr. Black?" Owen asked.

"Which one do you want?"

"Either will do."

"Good. I'm one."

"Mr. Black, I'd like to ask about a former employee of yours," Owen said. "His name is Robert Sanderson."

"Nope," Black said after he'd considered the name for a moment. "Doesn't work here."

"Are you sure?"

"Positive," said Black, tapping his head. "Eighty-two years old and never forget a thing."

"You're eighty-two?" Kate couldn't believe it. She'd have guessed at least a hundred. She wondered if there was a law prohibiting senile old men from operating food-related enterprises.

"Yes'm. Eighty-two years old and never forget a thing." He tapped his forehead again.

Owen looked at the paper in his hand. "Sanderson claims to have worked here until about eight months ago."

"Sanderson? Who's that?"

"Robert Sanderson? The man I asked about."

"Nobody here named Sanderson," Black said firmly.

"Owen," Kate whispered, "I don't think this is going to work."

The employees' door opened again and a slightly younger version of Black appeared. "Pop, do you need any help?"

"Nope," the older man said. "Eighty-two years old and got a mind like a steel trap."

The second man ignored his father's boast, wiped his hand on his blood-stained apron, and extended it to Owen. "Jack Black. Can I help you folks?"

Seeing no way to avoid it, Owen shook hands quickly. "Perhaps you can," he explained.

Jack Black's eyes narrowed when he heard Sanderson's name. "Pop, take a look in the back. You know how Artie gets if we don't watch him." Jack waited for his father to leave the room before he said. "Hell, yeah. I remember Sanderson. That no-good, conniving . . ." Jack stopped to take a deep breath. "Friend of yours?"

Owen shook his head.

"Good. He conned Pop out of a small fortune."

"*What?* How did he do that?"

Jack snorted. "Had him convinced he was buying oil wells in Texas. His scheme lasted six months before I found out. Why, I could have killed him!"

Kate started, but Owen went on smoothly. "How did he convince your father to hand over his money?"

"Sanderson told Pop he had all this Texas land, see. Claimed he'd inherited it as the last surviving member of some rich family. Claimed he didn't want to be a do-nothing rich kid. Said he wanted to work for his money. Naturally, Pop was impressed. So Sanderson said there was a lot of legal rigmarole that kept him from just giving his land away, but that he could sell it cheap. Turned out he was telling the same story to a few other folks 'round here, old uns mostly. Trying to convince them it was a great investment for their future, like they weren't one foot in the grave already."

"Did you report him to the police?"

"What the hell for? He was big buddies with the chief. That's how he knew which suckers to hit on. Used the police computers to look up their backgrounds and bank accounts and such."

"Well, thank you, Mr. Black." Owen nodded and began to back out the door.

"Yes, thanks," Kate said and followed him, trying to get out the door without touching it.

Once in the car, Owen began to laugh. "Imagine naming a kid Jack Black."

"Stop it, Owen. Don't you feel sorry for that poor old man?"

"Of course I do. But if it helps, just remember that Sanderson finally got himself killed. Probably for the same type of scam."

Kate's eyes widened. "You think he pulled this in Jesus Creek? Maybe we should talk to some of the older people. Although the wealthy ones *I* know wouldn't fall for such a blatantly obvious scam."

"It may not have been exactly the same story," Owen said, folding the résumé and tucking it in his pocket. "We'll update German, and he can see if any of these other employers have similar stories. I've had enough for today. Ready to head home?"

"Yes," Kate said. "And I'm becoming a vegetarian."

"Do you have any idea what kind of chemicals are sprayed on vegetables? Worse than anything in that warehouse, I can tell you."

"So what's safe to eat?"

"Nothing. And you might want to stop breathing, too. Just to be safe."

"Sarcasm doesn't become you."

"I'm just pointing out that, if one thing doesn't get you, the next one will. So stop piddling and get on with it."

"I'm not piddling."

Owen raised his eyebrows. "Really? What do you call it? Reading all those books that tell you how to think and how to live and—"

"Stop harping on my books!"

"How many have you read so far?" he asked. "Come on. How many?"

Kate flopped back in the seat and crossed her arms across her chest. "I don't remember."

"Maybe you should buy one about memory improvement."

Kate refused to respond. It had been a long day, and she realized that she and Owen were both just a little touchy. Come to think of it, every day of the past week had been long and frustrating and confusing. She leaned her head back against the seat and prayed for Monday to end.

CHAPTER 7

THE NEW MISS GOOBER ARRIVED FOR WORK on Tuesday wearing jeans and a tank top. She smiled and waved to one of the reporters who'd found his way back to the inn. Before going inside, she posed graciously for a few photos.

"Morning, Glenda." Kate looked up from the receipts that were spread out across her desk. "I wasn't sure you'd be back—now that you've won the pageant. Housework can't be very exciting to a beauty queen."

"Housework is never exciting," Glenda admitted. "I'm afraid I'll need some time off later. There's the state pageant in three months, and I'll have to spend days and days preparing for that. I have a great lady who's coaching me. State is where the pros do battle. I'll have to walk exactly right, and I'll need to practice interview questions."

"Practice answering questions?" Kate frowned. "Isn't that like studying for an IQ test?"

161

"You can do that, you know," Owen said. He'd just wandered in from the dining room, munching on a triangle of burned toast.

Glenda nodded in agreement. "We don't practice the actual questions," she explained. "Nobody's supposed to know those until the pageant. But there's a method. Like, if they ask, 'What's wrong with the world?', I have to say, 'Sure, there are a few problems, but things are getting better all the time.'"

Kate stared at her, thoroughly confused. "You didn't answer the question."

"No, but I gave a positive response. You must always be positive, no matter what they ask."

"Oh. It's like playing a game." Kate thought she understood the principle now. "But don't you ever get the urge to blurt out what you really think?"

"Heck, yeah. Everybody does. But if we all play by the same rules, it's as if everyone is telling the actual truth. Right?" Glenda flashed her pageant smile.

"I think what Glenda means," Owen offered, "is that truth is relative."

Kate looked from Owen to Glenda, trying to decide if they were putting her on. "Right," she said at last. "So, Glenda. We have to discuss Robert Sanderson."

"Who? Oh, that sleazy psychic. Sorry, Owen."

"I heard you were with him in Eloise's the night he disappeared," Kate said cautiously.

Glenda rolled her eyes. "Yeah. He caught up with me while I was jogging. I'll give him this much, he's a fast talker. Before I knew it I was stuck with him. He was babbling on about us sharing a life."

"Sharing a life? Was he proposing marriage, or explaining reincarnation?" Owen asked, obviously amused. "That's a pretty good pickup line. I never thought of using that one."

"And I hope you never will," Kate told him and turned back to Glenda. "Other than your adventures together in this other life, what did Sanderson talk about?"

"Who knows? Oh, he offered to help me win the pageant. I think he was leading up to some sort of bribe—like if I went to bed with him he'd put a spell on the judges or something. I told him I was already sleeping with every single one of the judges and couldn't fit him into my schedule."

"Glenda!"

"Relax, Kate." Glenda smiled. "Everyone assumes that about the winner anyway."

"If you say so," Kate said uncertainly. "Did he leave you alone then? Did he mention meeting anyone else?"

"You mean in this life? No, he just said he had business to tend to and he'd like to meet me later at my place. Fortunately, he forgot to ask where I lived. Just to be safe, I walked in the opposite direction until I was sure he was gone." Glenda started out of the room and up the wide staircase. "Can I clean his room, or have the police got it sealed?"

"They're finished," Kate called to her. "Go ahead." Turning to Owen she said, "Where in the world could he have been going that night?"

"Someplace nearby. Whatever he planned to do he didn't expect it to take long, or he wouldn't have made a date with Glenda."

"But where? Say, do you think he *could* have put a spell on the judges?"

Owen sighed. "Kate, for the last time, the man was not psychic. Even if he was, he couldn't have done that." He plopped down on the sofa and rested his chin on his hand. "He didn't expect it to take long. So how long does—"

"You know what's weird?" Kate said suddenly.

"The American political system."

"No," she said. "Well, yes. But if he was going to meet the person who killed him, and let's assume he was, he obviously didn't expect trouble. He didn't take anyone along to protect him. He didn't take a weapon."

"We don't know that. Maybe someone is walking around with a concealed wound. Or just possibly he meant to meet this person in a public place and didn't think it would be dangerous."

Kate considered it for a moment. "No. There's no public place in Jesus Creek open at that time of night except The Drink Tank. And German was there with a crowd."

Kate sat back down behind the desk and began to sort receipts into lopsided piles. She tried to imagine the life Sanderson and Glenda might have shared in the past. No doubt he'd have been a dashing knight and she the dragon who barbecued him.

* * *

"They found Lynne's clothes up there," Kate said, pointing toward the trees on the opposite bank. "That's where I took Carl yesterday."

"I thought German said she'd been in a cave." Owen squinted but still couldn't see anything except a hillside full of trees.

"It's the closest thing to a cave we've got. Up there. See the big oak? Oh, never mind. Just take my word for it."

"I will. What I don't understand is, why didn't the search team find her?"

"German says they searched the cave. Of course, true or not, he would say that. At any rate Lynne may not have gotten there until later. Or she may have been hiding from the searchers. You heard what she said on the tape. She was afraid she was being stalked, probably by her family."

Owen sat down on the creek bank and spread out a ragged quilt. It had been Kate's idea to have a backyard picnic rather than mess up the kitchen Mrs. Bradford cleaned so carefully every day. "This is a breathtaking view," he said. "You're lucky. You can step out the door and see this. God, what a great place for a kid to grow up. Have you always lived here? At the inn, I mean?"

"In this dump?" Kate looked over her shoulder at the backyard of the inn. Cardboard boxes, spare tires, and parts of an antiquated refrigerator littered the yard. Patrick had never found time to cart them off. "Patrick bought Twin Elms a few years ago. His wife's idea, really. She pictured it as a pastime. Restoring old homes is a très yuppie activity in Jesus Creek. I grew up a few houses down, though. In the respectable part of town."

"On the right side of the tracks?" Owen asked.

Kate nodded.

"Where's the wrong side?"

"Just across the creek there. See all those houses? That's Wicken Street. One man owns them all. He rents cheap, but he never repairs anything. And the tenants can't afford to pay for repairs. That's where Glenda lives, next door to the Bradfords. Her mother stays drunk all the time. That's probably why Glenda was out jogging the other night. One reason she's so determined to get through college is so she can buy a decent house that doesn't close in around her at night."

"A decent house doesn't necessarily bring happiness," Owen pointed out.

"But it helps. Those are the kids"—she pointed across the creek—"who wear clothes that never quite fit. I used to feel so sorry for them, especially the girls. You know how rotten kids can be to each other. Mary Beth Peters was one of my best friends, and she lived there."

"Friendship knows no social class. Mary Beth may not even have noticed that she was poor."

"Wanna bet?" Kate sat up and hugged her knees to her chest. "After school she used to collect Coke bottles and exchange them for pennies. There were five kids in the family, and they were all trying to save enough money for bus tickets out of town. To get away from the father who eventually beat Mary Beth's mother to death. Anyway, I went over there to visit her once and her father scared me so much

I never went back. My parents weren't crazy about my being there to start with. Mary Beth only visited my house once, too. For my tenth birthday party."

Owen watched the creek flowing under the walkbridge and finished off his bologna sandwich.

Kate went on. "Mary Beth was wearing dirty sneakers and a dingy, ruffled dress. You know, dressy but . . . hand-me-down. The other kids were just wearing school clothes, but they were so much nicer than her party dress. You could tell she was aware of the difference."

"Did Mary Beth give you a birthday present?"

Kate nodded. "A couple of comic books. Two of my favorites, in fact. *Fantastic Four* and *Magnus, The Robot Fighter*."

"And what did the other guests give you?" Owen asked.

"I don't know," Kate said. "I can't remember. Isn't that funny?" She reached out to pull a blade of grass that had been tickling her leg and noticed that her hand was trembling. "Her mother died right after that. Mary Beth just didn't show up for school one day, and I never heard from her again. And you know what else? When the teacher and my classmates started to wonder where she'd gone, I didn't say a word. See, I was the only one who knew about the bus tickets."

"Still got the comic books?"

"I wish I did." Kate kicked her feet in the creek and splashed water halfway across.

Owen handed her a sandwich, which she accepted absently. She hadn't thought about Mary Beth in years. Now she knew why.

Owen looked up sharply at the sound of a gun- shot in the woods directly across from them. "What's that?"

"Just kids," Kate said. "And idiots. They hunt out of season, in season, whenever."

"Violent little community. I wonder if Lynne had any kind of weapon."

"You sound like German. Do you honestly think she hauled around a baseball bat so she could clob- ber somebody?"

"That's not what I meant. But she spent time out in these woods. How could she have defended herself?" Owen shook his head. "And another thing—why didn't someone see her and alert the authorities."

"She could easily have stayed inside the cave during the day. When Carl and I were up there earlier, we saw the Bradfords out in their back- yard. I even called out to them, but they didn't see me until I drew attention to myself."

Owen turned to watch the water rippling past them. "A good place to hide, then? Hiding, when what she wanted was to find herself."

"Yes, but she wasn't hiding from herself. She was hiding from all the people forcing her to keep pre- tending she's . . . I don't know. Something she isn't, at any rate."

They finished their sandwiches silently, and Owen finally allowed himself to be dragged away from the creek when Kate pleaded self-defense. If the ledger wasn't ready for the accountant, Kate claimed, she'd be dead meat. "I swear. You can't imagine how intimidating this woman is. I think she's a beer-hall bouncer in her spare time."

"Okay, but you have to promise me a full-fledged picnic soon, with fried chicken, apple pie, and a tablecloth."

"You mean catered, of course."

Owen picked up the quilt and threw it over his shoulder, then turned to look once more at the row of shabby houses built along the creek bank. The sun beating directly down on the ragged roofs made every house along Wicken Street look hot and angry.

Mrs. Bradford was sitting on the front steps of the inn when Kate and Owen returned. She had her purse balanced on her knees and was staring straight out at the highway.

"It's almost one," Kate said, setting the picnic basket down on the porch beside her cook. "You should have gone home an hour ago."

Mrs. Bradford nodded slightly. "The reverend hasn't arrived to pick me up yet. I'd have walked, but we have business to take care of this afternoon so I have to wait."

"Well, at least wait inside," Kate insisted. "It's too hot out here."

"No thank you. The reverend will be by any minute."

Owen and Kate exchanged helpless glances. "Well, let me keep you company." Kate sat down on the porch. It was times like this she wished she weren't so softhearted. "Owen? Want to join us?"

"Okay." Owen draped the quilt over the picnic basket and settled comfortably on the other side of Mrs. Bradford.

"You know," Kate began, desperate for conversational material, "I was impressed with the reenactment. You and the reverend did an excellent job. I'm just sorry it . . . Well, that it ended the way it did." Somehow her friendly chat had gotten derailed.

Kate drew a deep breath of the sultry afternoon air, and tried to get back on track.

"What a terrible shock for you. But if you can just put this behind you, maybe we can reschedule the reenactment. For Thanksgiving, maybe."

Mrs. Bradford didn't respond. Hours rather than seconds seemed to drag by, until Kate finally threw a desperate glance in Owen's direction.

"Are you and your husband doing some shopping this afternoon?" Owen asked.

At last Mrs. Bradford moved, but only to turn her head and look sharply at Owen. "No," she said. "I have business to attend to."

As if on cue, Brother B.'s car turned into the driveway. It was a shiny blue number, practically new and spotlessly clean. When he approached the house Brother B. honked impatiently, as if he hadn't noticed that his wife had already risen and started out to the drive to meet him. As Mrs. Bradford climbed in the car, Brother B. rolled down his window and shouted greetings to Kate. "Hot today!" he yelled.

"You bet!" Kate shouted back. "I'm going in where it's cooler!" Kate rose and watched the Bradfords' car backing out toward the highway. "I wonder why he didn't just turn around up here and drive straight out," she said.

Owen looked up at her and said, "That forsythia bush over there." He pointed to the only area of the driveway wide enough for Brother B. to have used for a turn. "It would have scratched the finish on the car."

"Oh, it's just a little bush. It couldn't do that much damage, could it?"

"Some people are very particular about their cars," Owen said. He rose and held the door open for Kate, then gathered the picnic items and carried them inside. "I never understood why men get so passionately attached to their cars. Women don't."

"That's because women have a better grasp of reality," Kate said. "Cars die. Sooner or later, no matter what you do, cars die."

"Same thing goes for people," Owen pointed out. "But women get passionate about that."

On Wednesday morning Kate and Owen ate breakfast together. Sitting at a window table in the Twin Elms dining room, they watched thunderclouds line up in the sky. The promise of a cooling storm has caused everyone to perk up, Kate thought. Certainly her own disposition had improved. At least, until German interrupted.

"Howdy, folks," he said, bursting through the dining room door. Kate cringed. Today German was into his Marshal Dillon mode. He'd probably throw one leg across the back of a chair before he sat down. "Where's your reporter friend?"

"Out and about. Come to think of it, I never did hear him come in last night." Kate looked across at Owen. "Have you seen him?"

"Nope. Not me."

"He'll turn up eventually. Did you want to see him particularly, or will a cup of coffee suffice?" Kate made a conscious decision to be gracious today. She and Owen had had a lovely private conversation over breakfast and she now felt quite mellow.

The deputy remained in the doorway, adjusting his gun belt. Finally he said, "I need to talk to all of you. And I damn sure hope you've got airtight alibis."

"Oh for goodness sake, what's going on?" Kate had seen German's tough act plenty of times; it was getting old.

"I just came from the hospital. Somebody killed Lynne Hampton last night."

"*What?*" Kate asked weakly. It wasn't possible that she'd heard correctly.

German was still standing. "I said, Lynne Hampton's been murdered."

"That poor child," Owen muttered.

"I thought you had guards by her door! You swore you'd keep people out! *What happened?*" Kate's pitch was rising, getting shriller with every word.

"I had a guard to keep her in," German said levelly. "And don't you start in on me. The Hamptons are after my butt already."

"How?" Owen asked quietly.

"Somebody held a pillow over her face. Which means the best suspects are twenty different hospital employees. The only people who entered that room were nurses, doctors, and janitorial staff. And"—he added, looking straight at Kate—"your reporter."

"Oh, God," Kate said under her breath.

"Yeah. He got in the other night when Law was supposed to be on duty. Claiming to be a doctor."

"You might as well sit down," Kate told him. "How did you find out about Carl being there?"

German stopped, halfway into the chair. "You knew about it, didn't you, Kate?" he asked. His expression registered deep disappointment. "You should have told me."

"Never mind that. Carl didn't have anything to do with this. The question is: who else might have gotten into Lynne's room the same way he did?"

German nodded. "Most anybody, I expect. And the whole rest of this mess has gotten out of hand." German reached into his shirt pocket and pulled out a note pad. "Listen to this. That Sanderson guy. Besides taking that old geezer at the slaughterhouse, he also posed as an aluminum siding salesman in Nashville. Sold about thirty thousand dollars worth of siding to people, got their deposits, and left town. He was calling himself Johnny Jackson then."

"Why didn't someone catch him before this?" Kate wanted to know.

"Because he always hightailed it out of town first. And besides, people don't tell the police even when they've been fleeced. They get embarrassed, like.

Figure losing money is better than admitting they've been stupid." German shook his head, as if he couldn't imagine why anyone would mind being stupid.

"Anything else?" Owen asked.

"Four other towns that we know about so far," German said. "He had a different name in two of 'em, used Sanderson for the others. That's his real name, by the way."

"But that doesn't tell us anything about Lynne," Kate said. "Unless you think the same person—"

"I don't know what to think," German admitted. "Sanderson wasn't any of the people he claimed to be. And this Jackson—he claims to be a reporter. Hah! He's a"—German checked his notes—"a typesetter at the *Benton Harbor Sun*. Whatever the hell that is."

"Someone who types up newspaper stories," Owen explained. "But not someone who writes them, ordinarily. He might do both, though. You'll have to check with the paper."

"I did," German said. "They fired him three months ago. I swear to God, ain't nobody in this town who's what they're supposed to be."

They heard the front door slam, then the sound of shoes pounding across the bare wood floors. Carl burst into the dining room, talking at a fever pitch even before he was fully inside. "Lynne Hampton's dead. And I have the last interview she ever gave."

German whipped out his note pad and pencil again, then said, "Mr. Jackson, let's me and you have a talk."

* * *

Kate and Owen had been exiled to the study while Carl was being questioned. "Separating the suspect from his support group," German called it. Little did he know that Kate was leaning toward the side of the executioner.

"I'm furious with you!" she said as soon as she was alone with Owen. "You said no one else would get hurt, and now look what's happened! Lynne is dead! Why didn't you share your suspicions with German in the first place? Even if it was only a hunch, at least he might have done something."

Owen absorbed her criticism silently, but Kate continued to stare at him until he was forced to reply. "I talked to German and suggested he keep a guard on the girl. A real guard. I honestly thought she was safe, Kate. But something happened, something changed. I noticed it yesterday, but it didn't seem reasonable after all this time, so I just wrote it off as . . . well, as something else."

"Then at least tell German now. Tell him who you think the killer is. It can't hurt. After all, two people are already dead."

"And what do you suppose German will do? He'll either laugh in my face or go stampeding in like an elephant herd and run the killer right into the woods. Look, I'm going to find concrete evidence before I accuse anyone. Otherwise there will never be a way to prove anything I suspect, and no killer in his right mind is going to confess for the fun of it."

Kate rolled her eyes. "What killer is in his right mind anyway? Murder isn't exactly a sign of sanity."

"I guess not," Owen said quietly.

Kate knew his impulse was probably right, but she didn't want to apologize. She was upset and frightened, and at the moment Owen was the only person she could blame.

German pushed open the dining room door and made himself comfortable at their table. He spit into the tin can he'd brought with him, then shook his head. "What a mess. I've already had three calls from the Hamptons' lawyer. They're threatening to sue everybody."

"Well, they should. German, you were responsible for Lynne's protection." Kate was glad he'd come in. It gave her a target other than Owen.

"In the first place the guard was mainly to keep the girl in, not to keep other people out. And in the second place, and like I keep telling you, nobody out of the ordinary went into that room except Jackson."

"That you know of," Kate added. "Lynne was killed in the middle of the night and nobody noticed? How many people go into a patient's room in the night?"

"Now, look. The nurse checked her at midnight and she was sound asleep. There wasn't a reason in the world to check on her again. If the girl had needed anything, she'd have used her call button." German raised the can to his mouth and spit into it.

"Wait a minute," Owen said. "Lynne was asleep at midnight? Are you certain?"

German's mouth fell open, revealing a wad of chewed tobacco. "You reckon she was dead then? Naw, the nurse would have noticed."

"Would she?" Owen asked. "Did she actually speak to Lynne, fluff her pillow, take her pulse? Or did she just peek into a dark room and ascertain that there was a body in the bed?"

German shrugged. "I'll check. Sometimes folks on the night shift get a little sloppy."

Kate decided that was a classic example of a pot calling a kettle black.

CHAPTER

8

"DO YOU KNOW ANYTHING ABOUT PLUMB-ing?" Kate met Roger Shelton as he came through the front door of the inn. He was dripping from the rain that had bypassed his umbrella. Why is it, Kate wondered, that after weeks of heat and dust the rain breaks loose on the same day my water pipes do?

"Plumbing? Of course," he said. "What man doesn't?"

"Good. Then tell me what to do about the leak upstairs."

"Is there a leak? Well, the first thing you should do is call the water company."

"I did. They've turned off that thingamabob out in the front yard. Now there's no water in the inn, but at least it's not gushing all over the floor."

Roger gave her a brisk salute. "You've handled it, then. I'll just run upstairs and change. Did I mention that I have a date with Delia?"

"About four times, so far today." By conservative

estimate. "You've heard about Lynne Hampton, I suppose. German was over here this morning interrogating Carl."

"German has been everywhere interrogating everyone, including me." Roger looked quite pleased about this. "I don't think he wants to do that again. He seemed awfully upset by the time we were through."

"No doubt. But in this case I don't mind that you've probably twisted his brain into a pretzel. Did he ask you about the night Sanderson was killed?"

Roger shook his head. "No, I don't remember anything about that. Why? Does he think that has something to do with Lynne's death?"

Kate shrugged and leaned against the desk, thoroughly exhausted and fed up with the whole business. "It's just that you left here with Sanderson, and except for Glenda no one saw him alive again. I thought German might have decided that you'd killed him or something. You know how German is."

Roger nodded. His greatest regret was that German was entirely too dumb to be insulted. Roger took no pleasure in making fun of people who didn't know they were being made fun of. "Sanderson slipped by me. I was going to buy him a beer down at The Drink Tank, but he went to the bathroom and never came back. I wound up spending the better part of that evening listening to German and his reporter friends describe one gruesome murder after another."

"As long as you have an alibi," Kate said absently. "I'd hate for you to wind up in jail just when you're about to win Delia's heart."

"Sounds romantic to me. She could bake me cakes with files inside and visit me every other Sunday."

The door swung open and Patrick McCullough made his first entrance of the day. "Roger!" he said, as if delighted to see the man. "Glad to know you're still here." Patrick held out his hand but Roger ignored it.

"Patrick, thank God you're back." Kate took the extended hand and pulled Patrick around to face her. "I've been phoning everywhere for you."

"Well, I'm here now. Let me know when it's time for the evening news, will you? I just held a quick press conference about Lynne Hampton's death. Some of the Channel 4 news team were there."

"Never mind about press conferences," Kate said, batting a strand of hair out of her face. "There's no water."

"What do you mean, no water?"

"No water. I called the water company, but they said the problem's not theirs, it's ours. And they were right. There's a leak upstairs. A big one. The water company was magnanimous enough to shut it off outside so we won't drown. I think it's one of those pipes the plumber suggested replacing. The ones you said were too expensive to fix."

"Could be. I'm hardly a plumbing expert, Katherine. That means I won't be able to take a shower." Patrick checked his watch. "I'll go to Sheila's and freshen up there. Have to hurry, though, if I'm going to catch the newscast." He started out.

"Hold it right there." Kate reached out and

grabbed his arm, ready to restrain him physically if necessary. "Forget Sheila. What are you going to do about the flipping water?"

"I don't know. It seems to me if you've got the leak stopped, there's nothing else to worry about."

"We still need water for bathing and other such minor niceties. And we can't have it turned back on until the leak is fixed. Patrick, read my lips: we must call a repairman—now!"

"Okay," Patrick agreed. "Call someone. And Katherine, do something about your hair. You look terrible. Appearance is so important. I keep telling you that." Patrick chucked her under the chin. "Good to see you, Roger. Say, you've been in town quite a while now. Before long, you'll be a true citizen of Jesus Creek."

"I wouldn't go that far," Roger said.

"Well, don't forget to register to vote. You want a say in how your local government is run, don't you?"

"You bet I do," Roger said. "You bet I do."

"That's settled, then." Patrick turned back to Kate. "I'll grab a few clothes and pop on over to Sheila's. Just keep the show running, Katherine. You're doing great." He gave Roger a friendly pat on the shoulder and tore upstairs.

"I wonder if Delia would let me shower at her house," Roger said thoughtfully. "Hmm. Maybe if I told her that I can't sleep without a faucet dripping . . ."

"She'd give you a drip alright. Why don't you just change for your date and go on?"

Roger nodded. "Yes, and on my way I'll stop by

the courthouse to register. Never know when there might be an election."

Roger waited until he heard Patrick's door close, then gave Kate a crooked smile and went upstairs.

With her adolescent lovebird out of the way, Kate went to the phone and dialed Jack Gilbert, the only plumber in town. "It's Kate at the Twin Elms," she told him. "I think that pipe is shot. Yes, the one you mentioned before. Just replace everything you think needs to be repaired. Go over the entire house and fix everything."

She returned the receiver to the cradle, smiling. Then she pulled out a sheet of Twin Elms stationery and printed the date at the top. As she wrote out her formal resignation she noticed a pleasurable sensation in her chest, like a flock of doves escaping.

With Roger and Patrick out for the evening, Kate was grateful for Owen's company. Of course, she'd have enjoyed his company anyway. It would have been homey to lock the front door and start a fire in the fireplace, but that wasn't reasonable. For one thing Roger might come back anytime, especially if he didn't watch his behavior with Delia Cannon. And for another the temperature was still running in the high eighties, and Kate didn't think the new cooling system would hold up to a fire.

The second best choice was the breakfast nook. And that's where Kate and Owen retreated to eat pepperoni pizza and drink iced tea.

"I'm surprised at how conscientious German has become," Kate said. "Roger told me he's been questioning everybody in town about Lynne's death. Usually he just waits for information to come to him."

"Maybe he's shooting for a promotion," Owen said. "Or maybe he's worried about that lawsuit the Hamptons have threatened him with."

"Well, at least he's no longer blaming you for Sanderson's death. I wonder if he's planning to claim Lynne committed suicide because she couldn't live with herself after murdering him." Kate pulled a square of pizza from the box, wrapping the errant strings of cheese around it.

"German couldn't make that scenario work. Even though we may have underestimated him all this time. Maybe he's brighter than he looks."

"Ha!"

"You remember what he said the other day? That no one in this town is what he seems? He's exactly right."

Kate thought about it for a minute then said, "Okay. Sanderson wasn't you. But that's about it. Everyone else is regular."

"Not really. Consider this: you've got a maid who pretends to be a beauty queen; but she's really a scholar, right?"

"Right," Kate agreed. "But she's a beauty queen, too. And a darned impressive one."

"I agree. Still, that's not the real Glenda. The real Glenda cleans rooms and enters pageants only because she needs money for her scholarly pursuits."

"A degree in microbiology. Okay, maybe if you stretch it, that could be true." Kate nodded, more to herself than to Owen. She'd never considered it before, but Glenda probably wasn't what she seemed—at least not what she seemed to Kate, for Kate barely knew her.

"Your brother pretends to be a politician and an innkeeper and a salesman, right?"

"Right," Kate agreed. "And he's not fooling anybody."

"He's fools himself, which is all that matters. But what is he really?" Owen sat back in his chair, obviously expecting Kate to answer.

"I don't know," she said. "He's . . . well, he's just sort of Patrick. He's a social climber and a snob. Is that what you mean?"

"That's part of it."

"Well, at least we all know what I am," Kate said proudly. "I am the most honest, straightforward person you've ever met."

It was disturbing to watch Owen's face drop in amazement. "You're full of surprises, I'll say that. After all those books you've read—"

"Don't start on my books again."

"And you think you're not pretending? Come on, Kate. You've developed the most elaborate costume. You're always running around like a chicken with its head cut off, ranting and raving about the inn and the auction and all these things that you just can't handle. And then what do you do? You take care of it. You're probably the most competent person in town, but you refuse to admit it."

"That's nonsense. Why on earth would I pretend to be a nitwit unless I truly am?"

"Because airheads don't get asked to take responsibility, and if they don't have responsibility they can't screw up. And if they don't screw up, no one gets mad." Owen grinned. "You'd have paid a fortune for that if it had come from a therapist."

"I'd find it easier to believe, too. Well, let's not pick on everyone else until we've examined you." Kate propped her elbows on the table and looked across at Owen. "What are you, really?"

"Oh, me? I'm really a wealthy playboy. I just put on extra weight and live in a cheap apartment to make people think I'm just folks." His dimples were showing again.

The plumber had been kind enough to call at six-thirty A.M. to alert Kate that he'd be arriving at seven. He apologized for the late start. Kate dressed quickly and headed for the kitchen. Was that coffee she smelled? What had Mrs. Bradford made it with?

"Water supply," Mrs. Bradford said briskly, in response to Kate's question.

"What water supply?" Kate had heard of people stranded in the desert using water from their car radiators, but surely Mrs. Bradford hadn't siphoned the van's tank. Kate hoped she wasn't one of those people who use creek water, insisting that it purifies itself every twenty feet.

"I keep jugs of water in the freezer," the cook explained. "Never know when you'll need extra ice. Or water. And I wouldn't use that creek water the way some folks do. I don't care what they say. You never know what's in there."

Kate breathed a sigh of relief, remembering Sanderson's puckered corpse when they'd reeled it in.

"I wish I'd thought of that. Maybe I should keep a—" Kate suddenly remembered that in two more weeks, the water in this place would no longer be her problem.

"When's he leaving?" Mrs. Bradford asked suddenly.

"Patrick? I don't know. But before he does he'll have to hire—"

"No, not him. The psychic." Mrs. Bradford was beating muffin batter, her arm slapping against the side of her chest.

"I have no idea. Probably not until he finds Sanderson's murderer. And Lynne's. Assuming it's the same person."

"Hmph. I thought he was supposed to be all-knowing."

Kate poured herself a cup of coffee and sat down at the small kitchen table. Here's a chance to befriend an employee, she thought. Maybe dispel her silly notions about psychics. "Apparently he does know who the killer is, but he's reluctant to say until he figures out why it was done."

"That devil got what he deserved. That's what I say. The Lord will have his vengeance."

"It wasn't the Lord who killed Sanderson," Kate said. "It was some flesh-and-blood maniac."

Mrs. Bradford hurled the mixing spoon into the sink. "Got what he deserved," she repeated. "Coming in here, flaunting himself and his wickedness. Bringing trouble to good people."

"What you seem to have forgotten is that the man wasn't really psychic. He was a fake. Probably

couldn't have summoned up a spirit if his life de-
pended—well, he probably couldn't have."

"You don't have to belong to a union." That was
probably the closest Mrs. Bradford would come to
being humorous. Too bad she didn't know that's
what it was. "Cavorting with demons, that's the
Devil's work, whether he's an official psychic or not.
Folks got no business sticking their noses into
places the Lord keeps secret."

"Look, Mrs. Bradford, I need to tell you something. Could we just leave the subject of psychics,
real and otherwise, for a minute? I'm turning in my
resignation today. I'll only be here two more
weeks."

Mrs. Bradford's mind was elsewhere. Either that
or she was stunned to silence.

Kate went on. "I don't know if Patrick will decide
to stay home and run the place himself, or if he'll
hire someone. Chances are, he'll hire someone. If
you'd like, I'll suggest you for the job. The pay is a
little better, and I think you'd be good at the job."
Kate had stayed awake half the night considering
this idea. Cooking was not Mrs. Bradford's greatest
talent, and she was dreadfully miscast in her current role. But efficiency and organization—now that
she was good at. She could probably manage the
inn better than anyone else Patrick was likely to
find.

Mrs. Bradford carefully measured batter into
muffin cups. Scanty amounts, of course, but she'd
be equally sparing with expenses were she to manage the inn. "You're walking out on your brother
when he needs you most?" she asked. It was appar-

ent from her tone that she was greatly disappointed in Kate.

"He doesn't need me, Mrs. Bradford. He barely knows I'm here."

"Some people just don't know how to say it," the woman said sternly.

"Well he must be one of them, because he's never asked me to do anything. Just told me. And he's never said thanks either." Kate stood up and shoved the chair back under the table. "Now, do you want me to recommend you for the job or not?"

"I'd need time off for church and the like," Mrs. Bradford said, stopping to give Kate a stern look.

"I'm sure that could be arranged," Kate said briskly, and left the kitchen, acutely aware that what she had thought would be a kindness toward Mrs. Bradford had turned into something else altogether.

Jack Gilbert arrived promptly at seven, tool kit in hand. "This'll take a while," he warned. "Have to turn off the water."

"It's off already," Kate told him. "Someone from the water company took care of it."

"Oh yeah?" Jack didn't look happy about this invasion of his territory.

"I didn't have any other choice. I mean, there was water pouring across the second story floor, and I was afraid the lobby ceiling might collapse."

Jack looked up and considered the idea. "That'd be a sight, now. If you'd replaced those pipes when you were renovating, you wouldn't be having this problem now."

"I know, I know. But we certainly will take your advice in the future."

"I'd hope so. People sure can do a lot of damage when they get into areas they don't know about."

"Our cook was just telling me that, too."

Patrick bounced down the stairs, dressed in his favorite suit for traveling. He was carrying his suitcase. "Good, Katherine. You're up. There's no water upstairs. Oh hi, Jack. What brings you out our way?" Patrick stopped to shake hands with Jack, a registered voter.

"I thought you wanted me to fix a leak," Jack said defensively.

"Leak? Katherine, do we have a leak?"

"Yes, Patrick, we do," Kate said mildly. "But Jack can fix it. Nothing at all for you to worry about, Patrick."

"Great, great. Do it up right, Jack. It's heartening to know you're in charge." Patrick shifted the suitcase to his other hand and gave Kate a quick peck on the cheek. "See you in a few days."

"Going someplace?" she asked coolly.

"Didn't I mention it? I'm going to the conference in White's Bend. PR for Jesus Creek." He saw that Kate had no idea what he meant and tried again. "The Japanese businessmen who visited last spring are on the brink of deciding about a site for their factory."

"Oh, right," Kate said. "That was the front-page brouhaha in the *Headlight*. JAPANESE INVADE JESUS CREEK." Lindsay James Leach had not yet taken over the paper when that story ran, but the headline, not to mention the attendant article, was directly responsible for the termination of the interim editor. "Take along that issue of the *Headlight*. I'm sure they'd be impressed."

"I'm not taking anything. They scouted five places across the state, and there's not a chance in hell they'll pick Jesus Creek. I'm just attending the party on Saturday night."

"If they won't pick Jesus Creek, and if you aren't even going to make an effort, then why are you going?"

"The County Council has already approved a budget for it," he said simply. "No sense getting their records fouled up."

"Patrick, you were born to be a politician. But before you head out, let me just give you something to think about over sushi. Here." She handed him the envelope that contained her resignation.

"What is it?" he asked, and tucked it into his pocket without looking at it. "Can't you just take care of it?"

"I'm quitting, Patrick. That's my resignation. You have two weeks to find a replacement, and I'd suggest Mrs. Bradford."

"All right," Patrick held his free hand up in a gesture of surrender. "You want a raise? I can't blame you. No problem."

"Forget bribes, Patrick. Twin Elms and I are no longer a pair. That's it, so you'd better postpone your trip and scurry in there and interview Mrs. Bradford for this job."

Patrick gave her a smug grin. "A vacation, right? Fine, I'll even pay for it. How about Florida?"

"Read my lips, brother: I quit." Kate stood facing

him, determined to stare him down or faint from the effort.

"Okay, Katherine," he said at last. "I'll be back in a week, and if you haven't simmered down by then we'll work it out. Right now, though, I've got to run."

Kate watched him leave and wondered if he would remember to think about her resignation at all. She had worried that he might try to talk her out of it, and she'd worried even more that she might let him. But Patrick hadn't even taken her seriously. It should have made her angry, she realized, but instead she felt amused. By the time Patrick got back she'd have her suitcases packed and ready to go.

"So. Guess I'll get started now," Jack said. He made no apology for eavesdropping, but merely ambled off in search of leaky pipes.

Kate settled herself behind the desk and glanced out the window. The trees lining the walk looked especially green today, she noticed. The heavy rain the day before had washed them, and now they sparkled in the sun like jewels.

In fact now that she thought about it, everything looked brighter today. Maybe all the abnormal events lately had been the remnant of some strange dream she'd had, brought on by late-night pizza.

Glenda was coming up the front walk, dressed for work in her usual T-shirt and jeans. She fit perfectly into the landscape, like the goddess of the earth inspecting her handiwork.

"It's not hot," she said as she came through the door. "Can you believe it?"

"Rain," Kate said. "Probably the only one we'll get all summer. But it'll be hot this afternoon."

Glenda agreed. "Which is why I plan to finish up here this morning. I have to go over to Benton Harbor later, and I'd like to get started before we reach the boiling point. If I don't get everything done I'll come back tonight."

"You don't have to do that. Just finish up tomorrow." Kate was amazed at Glenda's energy and dedication. She never left any job undone. Of course, if Glenda had to choose between cleaning rooms or going home and spending an evening with her mother, Kate could see why work held such appeal for her.

"I've got to start picking out a wardrobe to take to State. My coach has some outfits that might fit me, so I'm going to try those on, see if they need to be altered. God, I hate this part of it." Glenda smiled and shook her head. "Actually, I hate all of it. But even if I don't win at State, there are scholarships for the first few runners-up. God willing, I'll be in school this fall and have most of this nonsense behind me."

"Can't you get a loan or a grant?" Kate asked. "It would be a lot easier."

"Yes, but first of all, those don't pay all the expenses. And second, I don't want to be constantly running from class to the financial aid office. If I get the money I need, enough to supplement a student loan, then I can stick it in an interest-bearing account and never have to worry about going broke just before I finish school."

"You really want this, don't you? It must be comforting to know precisely what you want, especially when you're so young. I'm almost twice your age and I haven't a clue about what I want."

"You're not twice my age," Glenda said. "Besides, you *want* to work here, don't you? I thought you did. Why else would you put up with it?"

"I guess I was just killing time," Kate said. "But I won't be here much longer. I've handed Patrick my resignation. In two weeks someone else will be running the inn, probably Mrs. Bradford."

"Oh, no! That old bat will drive us all crazy." Glenda sighed. "Well, at least I won't be here with her long. Maybe I can survive."

"Just try to think of a positive way to tell her to go jump," Kate suggested.

"Thinking of me?"

Carl had sneaked up on her. Having officially turned in her notice, Kate had spent the entire morning drinking coffee and gazing out the dining room window, indulging in fantasies about her future.

"Sorry to disappoint you, Carl, but I was thinking of almost everything except you."

"When's the water going to be fixed?" he asked, sprawling across a chair next to hers.

"Plumber's working on it now. Why don't you have brunch, on the house?"

Carl looked at her through narrowed eyes. "Is it poisoned? What's gotten into you? Why are you being nice?"

Kate smiled, "I feel very alive today, very generous. Because I'm breaking loose. Isn't it amazing how you can settle into a rut without even noticing? Without choosing it? Know what I mean?"

"No," Carl said. "I always know what I'm doing. I have a plan, everything written out. Nothing gets by me. For instance, I plan to have a Pulitzer by the time I'm forty."

"Oh, really?" Kate wondered if being a typesetter for *The Benton Harbor Sun* was part of his plan. Or getting fired from the job. Was that some clever scheme of his? "Is that something you can plan for? Doesn't someone else decide who wins the Pulitzer?"

"It's all in the execution. If it doesn't happen naturally, then I make it happen. I have the talent. All I need is to get the ball rolling and keep it on course."

"I guess modesty isn't a requirement for success," Kate said. "Never mind. I'm glad you're going to win the Pulitzer. I've never known a famous writer before."

"Be sweet to me and I'll let you fondle it. The award, I mean." He rose from the chair. "I want to get some shots of the room where Lynne died and talk to some of the nurses who were on duty. Find out what they saw."

"Hasn't it occurred to you that you're a suspect? After all, you sneaked into her room once. You'd better stay away from the place before you get yourself arrested."

"What is life without risk? Nobody is going to bother me. They wouldn't dare. I exude confidence."

Kate nodded. "You definitely exude something.

But I think you're scum for trading on Lynne's death. And you can forget about me ever buying a copy of that book."

"I'll give you a copy. Autographed." Carl blew her a kiss. "Sorry I can't stay for the free brunch. Maybe you can round up your chubby psychic and eat with him."

Kate smiled to herself. Poor Carl. He took himself so seriously. Well, she supposed someone had to.

When Brother B. arrived at noon to pick up his wife, Kate was in the kitchen. She had tried to avoid Mrs. Bradford as much as possible, since the woman insisted on throwing her a disapproving glance every chance she got. Unfortunately menus had to be approved, and Kate had to provide Mrs. Bradford with a signed check to pay for the next week's groceries and kitchen supplies.

"So you're going to be leaving us, Kate?" Brother B. asked. "I'm sorry to hear that. So many young people leave the homes of their fathers these days. I'd truly thought that you were going to stay here in your home for a lifetime." He shook his head and sighed heavily.

"This isn't my home, Brother B.," Kate pointed out. "This is Patrick's home—if you can call an inn *home*. But I've never been a part of Jesus Creek anyway. After all, I was gone for years when I was married to Tony. And I think I've fiddled around long enough. I have to start a life of my own, don't you think?"

"There's so much for families to learn, Kate—all

the things they used to know instinctively: loyalty, sacrifice. Have you ever considered, Kate, that your place on this earth may be right here at Patrick's side? You talk of starting a life of your own, but maybe this is the life God intended for you."

"I don't think so," Kate said. "But I'll give it some thought before I make any definite decisions. Has Mrs. Bradford told you that I've suggested she take my job here at the inn?"

Brother B. nodded. "Leora will be an excellent addition to your staff. She has all the qualities of a desirable employee. Much like those I mentioned in regard to families, Kate. The Lord has blessed me with an exceptional helpmate."

Purse tucked under her arm, Mrs. Bradford ducked her head modestly and joined her husband by the door. Now that he mentioned it, Kate could see that she was exactly the sort of wife Brother B. needed. Mrs. Bradford never spent money carelessly, thereby leaving the bulk of their income for his belongings: expensive cars and suits. The woman was strong as an ox, which meant she could do all the physical labor around their home and Brother B. would never have to get those expensive suits dirty. And best of all, Mrs. Bradford adored her husband and would never, ever complain about the grossly unjust situation.

"You are lucky," Kate said sincerely. "And Patrick will be lucky to have Mrs. Bradford running the inn. She'll do a much better job of it than I have."

Brother B. reached out and put one arm around his embarrassed wife, squeezing her hard. Despite his wide smile and enthusiastic embrace, he still seemed to be playing the role of Hiram Wicken. Kate had the feeling he would have hugged anyone who happened to be standing next to him at the moment, as if Mrs. Bradford were only one more sheep in the flock he tended.

By late afternoon Jack had begun to whistle. Kate took that to mean he'd either found the problem and expected to solve it easily or else he'd decided to live in the woods with his six short brothers.

She wandered into the study, where she spotted Owen. He'd laid claim to a comfortable chair and was flipping through a magazine. "What have you been up to?" she asked as she crossed to her desk.

"I went all over town this morning, talking to people and trying to get new input."

"Poor old Carl is wandering around, too. He hopes to get permission to photograph Lynne's hospital room."

"Probably won't be worth the effort if he does get in. Have you seen that cheap camera he uses?"

"What?" Kate couldn't believe her ears. "You're a camera snob?"

"I'm not being snobbish about his dime-store camera. But if he has an amateur's camera, I assume he's an amateur photographer. The kind who takes *snapshots*." Owen said it as if the word were an obscenity.

"Owen Komelecki, you are a *snob*! I guess you can never really know anyone."

"I can, but that's my job." He rose from the love

seat and sauntered across the room to Kate's desk. "What's that you're writing?"

She covered her things-to-do-before-moving list with one arm and picked up a sealed envelope. "Well, snob, I don't know if I should give you this after all."

"What is it?" Owen asked, taking the envelope carefully between two fingers.

"My résumé."

Owen's eyebrows shot up. "Are you looking for a job?" he asked with a grin.

"Yes," Kate said. "I am." Well, so much for his claim that he knew people. It was obvious that Owen Komelecki had been taken completely by surprise.

He tore open one end of the envelope and pulled out the typed paper inside. "Hmmm . . . experience in business management, bookkeeping, customer relations," he read aloud. "This is certainly impressive, Miss Yancy."

"That's *Ms.*," she corrected him.

"Sorry. I need someone who can handle the office when I'm gone. I haven't always been this picky, but a close personal friend suggested I be more careful about the people I hire. Can you handle responsibility?"

"I'm very experienced at running a business," Kate said, watching him intently.

"And you're a confident woman, too. I can tell by the way you've requested a ridiculously high salary. But do you know anything about photography?"

"Not yet," she admitted. "But I'm a fast learner

and I've got this." She held up a paperback copy of *The Complete Photography Handbook*.

Owen shook his head. "I'm sorry. I have a very strict rule about that. I never hire people who use textbooks."

Kate's mouth flew open, but none of the words in her head reached her tongue. Which was probably just as well. She was still groping for a snappy retort when Carl slammed through the front door.

"Here!" Kate said, and tossed the *Photography Handbook* at him. "And while you're at it, get rid of that cheap camera."

"Very good," Owen said approvingly. "A bit drastic, but certainly a step in the right direction. You're hired."

CHAPTER 9

KATE AND OWEN WALKED THE HALF MILE from Twin Elms Inn to the courthouse square, where German's patrol car was parked. It was barely eight A.M., but Owen had been pacing the study since before six. He'd wanted to go then, but Kate had finally convinced him that German would not officially open up the police department until later, and that the night dispatcher would have the door locked until at least seven.

"I don't know why I didn't think of it before," he kept muttering. "It was right there. When we found those files, I should have known."

"Either make sense or hush," Kate told him.

They found German finishing his breakfast coffee and bear claw behind the cluttered desk, his feet propped on a pile of half-written reports.

"Morning," German said through a mouthful of pastry. "What can I do you for?"

"I need to know everything you've found out

about Robert Sanderson. Particularly what he did just before he died."

German leaned back in his chair and pulled a pouch of Red Man from his shirt pocket. He took his time shoving tobacco into his mouth, determined to proceed according to his own tempo, not Owen's. Finally he admitted, "We don't know anything new about his movements that night. But we sure got the story on what he'd been doing up until he hit Jesus Creek."

"Has he ever used Owen's name before?" Kate asked.

"Not that we can find out. But he used a lot of others, and far as I can tell he never did an honest day's work in his life. We're still getting in reports on him. I swear, I think he's pulled something in every state in the country." German picked up his Styrofoam cup, drank the last of the coffee, then stuffed a Kleenex in the cup. "What I can't figure out is how come nobody's killed him before this."

"I particularly wondered about those files he had in his room," Owen said. "Do you have any idea how he got that information? Not the news clippings, but the items about Kate, for instance."

"He worked for you, didn't he?" German asked.

"Yes, but—"

"Got a computer in your office?"

Owen shook his head. He was proud of his computer-phobia and considered himself the last holdout against technological tyranny.

"Well, then. Have you ever heard of a hacker? He came in here right after he got to town, spent half a morning playing with this one here." German pointed to the new computer tucked away in the corner of the room. "What do you suppose he was doing with it?"

"I give up," Owen said wearily. "Playing video games? Wiping out a bank somewhere?"

German grinned, satisfied at having found something he knew that Owen didn't. "According to my sources, Sanderson would use NCIC files and court records to dig up dirt on a lot of his victims. Then he'd use them either to convince people he knew all about them because God had told him, or he just plain blackmailed them. He picked up info about the good folks here in Jesus Creek just that way."

"And you let him use your computer to do that?" Kate asked.

German sat up straighter and tried to look like an honest cop. "He did it when I thought he was the Hamptons' employee. I didn't have a reason in the world to suspect him of anything worse than nuttiness."

"Can you show me how to use that thing?" Owen asked with a sigh. Some things could be avoided only so long, and Owen seemed resigned to his fate.

"You kidding?" German scratched his head. "Actually, Sanderson wrote the instructions down for me when he was in here. They're around somewhere."

"You don't know how to operate your own computer?" Owen was clearly beginning to get impatient.

"In the first place, I grew up in this town. I already know all there is to know about folks around here, so I don't have to ask no damn computer. And in the second place, if I want to know something that I don't already I just call up NCIC, like we always did back before the whole world went computer-crazy."

"You call on the phone? Would they have the same information that's on the computer?"

"Where do you think the computer gets it?"

Owen smiled. "German, why don't you give them a call right now?"

"Sure. But what are we asking about?"

"You dial. I'll explain."

Kate thought she at least owed Eloise a decent farewell, so she'd planned ahead. The breakfast rush at the diner was always over by eight-thirty, since most customers had to be at work by nine. She'd been looking forward to having this breakfast with Owen, but he and German had gotten involved in their telephone call and Kate had wound up slipping out the door without either of them noticing.

"So you finally wised up!" That was Eloise's delighted comment when she learned of Kate's resignation. "I wondered how long it would take you. And what are you going to do now? Leave town, I suppose."

"Have to. I've got a new job." Kate bit slowly into her bacon sandwich, realizing it would be one of the last she'd have at the diner. "I can't say I hold out much hope of making my fortune at it."

"Don't tell me. You're going into the psychic business?"

"Maybe *you* should," Kate said. "You're right in

a way. I'm going to work as Owen Komelecki's assistant. Trouble is, he usually goes through about four or five of them in a year."

"Kiddo, I predict you'll last the stretch."

"So I'm leaving you to deal with Carl. How are you doing with him? I hope this isn't going to be serious. I'd hate to think of you stuck with him for the rest of your life."

Eloise laughed and tossed her hair. "You've got to understand, there's a difference between a man to have fun with and a man to stick with. Carl's a jerk. You know that. But he's cute, and I'll just bet he's a lot of fun."

Kate shook her head. "You make me feel like Mrs. Bradford. All stuffy and prudish."

"Not a chance. There couldn't be more than one of her in the world. Or we'd all be wearing long dresses and pulling our hair back and making prune lips all the time."

Kate nodded. "I've often wondered what the woman does when she's not at work. Do you think she ever watches soap operas or reads romance novels?"

"No way. She mostly follows Brother B. around, catering to his every whim. And of course, she does her Christian duty. Visiting the shut-ins, making sick rounds at the hospital."

"Good heavens. Wouldn't she make a sick person want to get on his feet again? Just so he could get out of her path . . ."

"No kidding." Eloise lit a long brown cigarette and blew smoke out in perfect circles. "Last night I was there to see Aunt Iris. She broke her hip, you know, and I always go and sit with her until she drops off to sleep. The nurses have about had it with her."

"I'm sorry. I thought your aunt was doing much better lately," Kate said.

"She never does any better. Whiniest woman I ever saw."

"Did Mrs. Bradford come in to see her, too? No wonder Aunt Iris is so grumpy."

Eloise shook her head. "No, Brother B. came in, but he didn't stay long. He went on across the hall to visit Harvey. They split up, so they can hit twice as many rooms twice as fast. They don't seem to enjoy it much, anyway. I guess they just do it 'cause it's sort of expected, you know."

"Harvey the drunk? What's he doing in the hospital?"

Eloise shrugged. "Hurt himself working on the Bradfords' roof. He does odd jobs for them now and then."

Kate stopped eating for a moment. Wait a minute, she thought. The Bradfords had been at the hospital last night. Had they been there earlier in the week? And Harvey worked for them on occasion. "Eloise, do you sit with Aunt Iris every night?"

"Sure," Eloise said. "Who else is gonna do it?"

"Were you there Tuesday night?"

Eloise nodded.

"And what about the Bradfords? Were they there that night, too?"

Eloise reflected for several seconds before she answered. "Oh, yeah. I remember, because I'd just left Aunt Iris for a minute. I have to take a break from

her every now and then. And Larry Law was sitting outside that girl's room."

"Lynne's? I think German mentioned he was
supposed to be on guard duty that night."

"Right. Anyways, him and me go back a long
way. You know how it is. He hasn't aged well,
though. I think I liked him better with the beard.
So on my way out I stopped and talked to him for
a minute. He said sitting there was just about the
dullest job he'd ever had. Guess he felt different
when they found out that girl had died right under
his nose."

"Did you and Larry go for coffee or anything?"
Kate asked. A picture was forming in her mind, but
the edges were still blurred.

"As a matter of fact I was just thinking of asking
him to come on over to my place after he got off,
but just then old lady Bradford came out of the room
and that sort of turned my thoughts away from
earthly pleasures. Know what I mean?"

"Mrs. Bradford was actually in Lynne's room?
Are you sure Brother B. wasn't in there with her?"

Eloise tapped one long red fingernail on the
counter while she tried to remember. "I guess he
might have been, but I really wasn't paying attention."

"But Lynne was okay when Mrs. Bradford left?
Did you see her?"

"Heck, no. I've always hated people who go
around peeking in hospital rooms. Makes the patient feel like somebody in a freak show. But I know
she was all right, because Mrs. Bradford told Larry
she'd finally got the poor girl to sleep. She'd been

raising a real fuss there for a while, hollering and carrying on." Eloise shook her head. "Wouldn't you, if Old Lady Bradford was trying to save your soul?"

"Eloise, you're in the wrong business. Maybe Owen should hire you instead of me."

Kate had hurried back to the police department, only to find that Owen had left without her.

"He said something about going over to the Bradfords," German told her. "He asked a lot of questions about Brother B., and then he took off."

"Good Lord!" Kate gasped. "Alone? Let's get over there before all hell breaks loose!"

German reluctantly followed her outside to the patrol car. "What on earth are you talking about? He just wanted to ask them about that business over in Liberty City."

"Get in," she ordered, sliding into the passenger seat.

"Are you sure you know what you're doing?" German had opened the driver's door and was peering in at her.

"Damn it, German, let's go!" Kate's voice was louder than she'd intended. She noticed, too, that her heart was thudding and her throat seemed to have swollen shut.

"All right," German grumbled, getting in behind the wheel. "But you folks sure are making a fuss about a little missing money."

"Money? German, what are you talking about? Brother B. is a killer. He murdered Lynne and probably Sanderson, too."

"What?" German snorted. "Give me one good reason why Brother B. would kill anybody."

"I don't know why he killed Sanderson," Kate admitted. She was pressing her foot into the floor of the patrol car and at the same time urging German to hurry the hell up. "I also don't know why he killed Lynne, or why he had Harvey try to kill Owen and me. Owen knows, though, and he's over there alone. For God's sake, why didn't you go with him?"

"Well, I was going to. But I got a call about Harley Jones shooting at trespassers again. You know how he is when he takes one of these spells. One of these days he's actually gonna hit somebody."

"I do not care about Harley Jones," Kate said stiffly. "Will you hurry please?"

"There's Brother B. now," German said, pulling into the Bradford's driveway.

Brother B. had arrived just ahead of them and was getting out of his car with a big smile on his face. He seemed puzzled when he noticed Kate in the patrol car, but he waved just the same. "Always good to see you both. Will you come in for a while?"

The houses along Wicken were in even worse shape than they had been the last time Kate had visited the area. Most of them were sagging in the middle and a few sat up off the ground, their foundations nothing more than four stumps, one set at each corner. Still, the Bradford house looked almost respectable. In sharp contrast with the cluttered yards of the neighbors, this one had a freshly cut lawn, and a few marigolds grew at carefully spaced intervals along the driveway. The window shades were all drawn to the same level, Kate noticed, making the windows resemble a bunch of half-closed eyes.

Kate jumped from the car and demanded, "Where is he?"

"Where's who?" Brother B. asked.

"Owen. What have you done to him?"

"Brother B., why don't we all go inside and get out of this heat? Kate's got some crazy idea about you, and we need to straighten it out."

Brother B. shrugged. "Well, sure. Come on in and I'll have Leora fix us some tea. She'll be tickled to see you both."

Brother B. led them through the living room to the kitchen. "Leora!" he called. "We've got guests." Seeing grocery bags still on the table he muttered, "Funny. She must be around here somewhere. This milk's going to spoil if she doesn't get it put up soon." Kate noticed with grim amusement that Brother B. didn't bother to put away the milk himself.

"Never mind," Kate said. "We want to know where Owen is."

"Mr. Komelecki? I'm afraid I can't help you. Is there any reason you think he'd be looking for me?"

German leaned across the table for a bag of chocolate cookies, opened it, and began eating. "Brother B., you know I think real highly of you. But there is a matter to clear up. Why don't you explain to us what happened to that money in Liberty City?"

"Forget money," Kate said. "Where's Owen?"

Brother B. had turned pale and was staring at

the floor. "Well," he said at last, "I guess the truth will tell."

"It certainly will," Kate said. "We know all about you killing Lynne and Sanderson. Now what have you done to Owen?"

"Now, Katie," German mumbled, his mouth full of cookie, "let's not be slandering a man of God."

"Kate, I swear to you"—Brother B. gave her a pleading look—"I had nothing to do with killing anyone."

"You expect me to—" Kate was interrupted by the sound of a gunshot that shook the windows in the tidy kitchen.

"What the hell?" German said, and jumped up from the table, catching his gun belt on the edge.

Kate had already started out the back door. There had been no time, not even an indecisive second, to wonder about the sound. She'd known immediately that the shot had come from the backyard and that Owen was in danger.

Once in the yard, though, she was stunned by the sight that confronted her. Mrs. Bradford was on the ground, rolling frantically from side to side while Owen sat astride her, trying to pin down her flailing arms.

"Leora!" Brother B. shouted. He pushed his way past Kate and stalked into the yard. "What will people think?"

Owen and Leora Bradford both stopped in midstruggle and looked up at him. Then Owen began to laugh, as he rolled clear of Mrs. Bradford. He got to his feet, carefully picked up the gun that lay on the ground, and handed it to German without a word. He was dusty, sweaty, and gasping for breath, but Kate hugged him anyway.

"What the hell's going on here?" German demanded.

Owen pried himself loose from Kate and turned to German. "Mrs. Bradford will explain," he said. "If she doesn't, I will." This was obviously meant as a warning.

"I thought you were dead," Kate whispered.

"You must've been reading my mind," Owen told her. "I thought I was dead, too."

"That's not funny." Kate swatted his shoulder, then wiped a tear from her cheek.

"Darned right it's not. It was only my catlike reflexes that saved me."

"Would someone please tell me what's going on?" German demanded.

He looked at Mrs. Bradford, who was standing defiantly in the middle of the yard. She clearly had no intention of explaining anything. Brother B. was watching her nervously, but he made no effort to go near her.

"Okay," Owen said. "I guess I'll have to do it. These two are responsible for Sanderson's murder."

"Just a minute," Brother B. interrupted.

"I know you didn't kill him," Owen said, raising one hand for silence. "Brother B. here just whacked Sanderson with a shovel. Mrs. Bradford made that very clear to me. She's determined that the good reverend not be blamed for anything."

German was listening with his mouth wide open. "You got to be kidding me," he said.

"And after Brother B. knocked him out, Mrs.

Bradford finished the job. She didn't want Sanderson coming to and having her husband arrested for assault." Owen turned to look at Mrs. Bradford, disgust showing on his face. "It takes pretty steady nerves to beat an unconscious man until you've crushed his skull, doesn't it?"

Mrs. Bradford glared at him, but didn't speak. She'd obviously seen enough TV cop shows to know that silence was her best bet.

"And it takes a gutless wonder to let his wife do something like that, just to cover his own crime," Owen went on. "I suppose everything would have been fine if Kate hadn't taken Carl Jackson over to the cave. She saw the Bradfords in their backyard that day, and even shouted to them to let them know she was there. That's when it occurred to Mrs. Bradford that Lynne Hampton might have seen her kill Sanderson. Right?"

Mrs. Bradford showed no emotion at all, but at least her husband had the good grace to flinch. "Leora," he said, "you sure made a fine mess of things."

Owen handed Kate a cup of coffee, then sat down beside her at the table in the breakfast nook. "I told you it would only get worse," he said.

Kate nodded. "You can't begin to imagine what this is going to do to Jesus Creek. Every member of that church will be devastated."

"I know. And it's all been caused by the stupidest thing. Brother B. made personal use of some church funds over in Liberty City. That's what I learned from German's phone call this morning. And of course, Sanderson had found out about it. The church there didn't even pursue it. They just had him resign."

"And then he came here and started the Traditional Faith Church. But I don't understand why Sanderson confronted him in the first place."

Owen shrugged. "According to Mrs. Bradford, Sanderson wanted more than money this time. She said he threatened to make a general announcement to the congregation unless Bradford resigned here, too. Apparently Sanderson was going to step in and take over as head of the church."

"But he was supposed to be a psychic. Why would anyone fall for that? He didn't even have credentials. He didn't even have his own name, as far as that."

"I suppose he was counting on the Bradfords' support to help him win over the church membership. With a job like that, plus whatever little scams he was running on the side, he'd have lived well enough. And nobody would have bothered him about all those past cons. Who suspects a preacher of breaking the law?"

"She tried to kill us, too, you know. That day Harvey nearly ran us down with his truck."

Owen nodded. "Yes. When I confronted her, she started cursing Harvey for his sloppy workmanship. She'd apparently offered him a month's worth of Jack Daniel's if he'd kill me. Needless to say, she didn't pay off."

"You know what gets me?" Kate said. The coffee Owen had poured for her was getting cold. "The way he stood there and let Mrs. Bradford take the blame. If Brother B. hadn't attacked Sanderson, none of this would have happened. And then when his wife tried to help him, he just threw her to the wolves."

Owen nodded. "But you notice, she didn't seem to mind. She's used to covering for him. That's her job."

"Someone should straighten her out," Kate said, almost in sympathy. "But I guess it's a little late for that."

"It wouldn't matter. Her entire existence depends on him, on being the reverend's wife. That's who she is. Without that she would probably just dry up and blow away. That's the trouble with fabricating an identity. It can't hold up forever."

Kate sighed and leaned back in her chair. "But everybody has to be somebody. Maybe that's exactly what Mrs. Bradford *is*, and if that's so, it's not her fault. She has to be herself."

"Herself . . . But she doesn't even know who that is. She picked a persona. She tried to become what she thought would gain her respect and admiration. And you see what happened."

"Yes," Kate admitted. "But she was doing the best she could."

"Uh-huh," Owen said. He reached across the table to take Kate's hand. "Don't we all?"

"God! You just can't tell about anybody anymore. Even the preacher . . ." Kate shook her head. "You know, I try to be a nice person. I try to respect others and trust people, but that's such a dangerous way to live."

"Kate?" Owen said.

"Yes?"

"Live dangerously."

About the Author

DEBORAH ADAMS is an award-winning poet and short story writer. Actively involved with Sisters in Crime, the Appalachian Writers' Association, and other writers' organizations, Ms. Adams lives in Waverly, Tennessee. ALL THE GREAT PRETENDERS is her first novel—and she has completed a sequel: ALL THE CRAZY WINTERS.

MYSTERY
in the best 'whodunit' tradition...

AMANDA CROSS
The Kate Fansler Mysteries